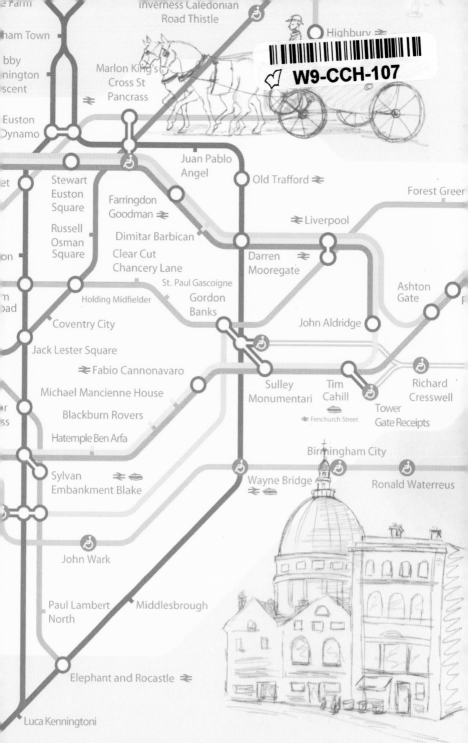

Fram

ham Town

bby
nington
scent

Inverness Caledonian
Road Thistle

Highbury ≷

Euston
Dynamo

Marlon King's
Cross St
Pancrass

≷

et

Stewart
Euston
Square

Juan Pablo
Angel

Old Trafford ≷

Forest Greer

Farringdon
Goodman ≷

≷ Liverpool

on

Russell
Osman
Square

Dimitar Barbican

Clear Cut
Chancery Lane

Darren
Mooregate

≷

Ashton
Gate

m
oad

St. Paul Gascoigne

Holding Midfielder

Gordon
Banks

John Aldridge

Coventry City

Jack Lester Square

≷ Fabio Cannonavaro

Sulley
Monumentari

Tim
Cahill

Richard
Cresswell

r
ss

Michael Mancienne House

Blackburn Rovers

≷ Fenchurch Street

Tower
Gate Receipts

Hatemple Ben Arfa

Birmingham City

Sylvan
Embankment Blake

≷ ⛴

Wayne Bridge

⛴

Ronald Waterreus

John Wark

Paul Lambert
North

Middlesbrough

Elephant and Rocastle ≷

Luca Kenningtoni

cky Stockwell

Mira's Diary

Text and illustrations copyright © 2014 Marissa Moss
Cover and internal design by Simon Stahl
Original series design by Liz Demeter/Demeter Design ©2012 Sourcebooks, Inc.
Cover design concept by Brittany Vibbert, Sourcebooks

Published by Creston Books, LLC in Berkeley, California
www.crestonbooks.co

CIP data for this book is available from the Library of Congress.

Source of Production: Worzalla Books, Stevens Point, Wisconsin
Printed and bound in the United States of America
1 2 3 4 5

For Steve Geck, who helped teach Mira
the ins and outs of time travel.

BOMBS OVER LONDON

Mira's Diary

BOMBS OVER LONDON

By Marissa Moss

Creston Books

July 8

We hadn't been in Rome long, but I'd already fallen totally in love with the city. The golden light on the ancient stone walls, the bright white dome of Saint Peter's floating high above the other buildings, the charming cobbled streets where handsome Italians dashed by on motorbikes. So I was torn when a postcard from Mom came for us at our hotel. I wanted to explore the city, but I wanted to find Mom even more. She had been gone now for seven months – or several centuries, depending on what measure of time you used. The regular, everyday kind or time travel years which fold back and forth like an accordion.

Somebody should invent a watch that shows them all. It would look something like this:

If I had a device like that, I wouldn't have to rely on her postcards. If Mom was in third-century Morocco or in twelfth-century Mongolia (which I fervently hoped she wasn't), I'd know exactly where and when to find her. Because Mom hadn't gone missing all those months ago, she'd gone time traveling, trying to change the past so that some Horrible Thing wouldn't happen to our family in the future. And, even more astonishing, I could time travel too. The first time (okay, pun intended) was in nineteenth-century Paris, and now I'd just gotten back from sixteenth-century Rome. I'd tried to help Mom make the changes she thought would work, the ones that would put events on a different track so the Horrible Thing wouldn't happen to us after all. It was all much trickier than you might think, trying to blend in when you belonged to a different culture, country, and, oh yeah, time. And then on top of that, I had to figure out what to change and how to do it.

The first clue always came in a postcard. Quaintly old-fashioned, come to think of it. The desk clerk handed it to Dad along with our room key when we got back from a dinner of pizza so thin and light, you had to use a knife and fork to eat it.

"It's from Mom!" Dad cheered, waving it in front of him.

"Where's it from?" asked my older brother, Malcolm. "Where are we going?"

Dad smiled like he'd won the lottery. I wondered what that meant, what city he'd wished for. I had my own wish list. I closed my eyes and crossed my fingers. "Madrid," I whispered. "Istanbul. Hawaii." All places I wanted to go.

"What are you muttering?" Malcolm elbowed me. "Why are your eyes closed?"

"Let's get back to the room and then we can talk about this," Dad said.

The elevator was old and slow. Dad had the postcard tucked into his shirt pocket and refused to say anything more about it. As if the Swedish tourists who got out on the second floor would have understood what we were talking about. Malcolm jiggled his leg nervously the whole way up. I could see he was itching to snatch the postcard, but he managed to control himself. I kept up my whispered chant – Madrid, Istanbul, Hawaii, Madrid, Istanbul, Hawaii.

"Stop it," Malcolm hissed. "I know what you're doing and you'll jinx us. We'll end up in Kazakhstan, Kurdistan, or some other horrible -stan."

"Why the hush-hush stuff?" I asked Dad as he opened the door to our room. "Are you worried that the Watcher is after us here?" I'd only seen the Watcher chasing after Mom in the past. I'd never seen her in the present. It was scary to think she could be looking for us here.

"Mom's breaking some important Rules and so are we. That means we should be careful."

With the door safely closed behind us, Dad presented the postcard with a grin and a formal bow.

"London!" Malcolm hooted. "Pip-pip, cheerio, and all that, old boy!"

London! Was that good or bad? It wasn't Madrid, or Istanbul or Hawaii, but at least we didn't have to go China or any -stan country. I wasn't sure how I'd manage in places like that. Plus going to London meant I'd be speaking the right language, if you considered American English a close relative to British English. And it would be a civilized country, with tea and cake and manners. Although when I thought of London, I pictured Mr. Bean and marmite and bad teeth.

Dad flipped over the postcard dramatically and read it out loud:

> Dear David, Malcolm, and Mira,
> I need to try again to make things right. My next chance for that is here. Mira, you need to find Room 40, Admiralty Building in Whitehall. Once you do, you'll know what it is that has to change.
> Love you all and hope to see you very soon!
> Serena (Mom)

"That's the most specific Mom's ever been." Malcolm almost sounded worried, like it was a bad thing. "Usually she points you to a person."

"Maybe she wants to help me more, for once. She says 'next chance.' Does that mean there are several more chances and she'll keep on trying until I get things right?" Which was good because I could get better and finally bring Mom home, but also bad, because if I didn't succeed, I'd be doing this forever. Mom wasn't the kind of person to give up on anything easily. Dad called her "doggedly determined," meaning once she started something, there was no stopping her. Dinners had burned, bathtubs had overflowed while Mom was focused on some computer problem from work. We'd joke that she was absent-minded, but really she was the opposite, so intensely focused on whatever she was doing, the rest of the world didn't exist.

Dad gave me a look that said Don't Get Your Hopes Up. He knew Mom's stubbornness better than anybody. He claimed he'd never won an argument with her about the things she really cared about. So, sure, he could pick the car they bought or what color to paint the backyard fence, but not anything to do with us, from our names to how to spend summer vacations. I had to admit, I was glad Mom won those fights, since Dad wanted me to be Estelle and Malcolm to be Joel. He wanted to give grandparent names to babies!

I picked up the postcard, studying it for clues. How old was the stamp? I wondered. It didn't tell me anything, but Malcolm would be better at figuring out stuff like that. "When was Big Ben built? That could mean something."

"Or not," Dad said. "You didn't go back to medieval Paris when we got a gargoyle postcard, or to ancient Rome when the postcard was of the Colosseum."

Good thing too! Who wanted to deal with gladiators or the plague? I handed the card to Malcolm. "If Mom's talking about the Admiralty Building, it can't be medieval, right? Or Renaissance? I'd rather go to a time when there's indoor plumbing."

"I agree, you need a time when there are showers, so you don't come back reeking." Malcolm waved away my imaginary stench. (I'd showered that morning for a good, looooong time!) He wasn't keen on sixteenth-century Roman hygiene or the lack of it, and to be honest, neither was I. Admiralty sounded modern though. Or at least not too ancient.

"Mom is what matters, getting her home." Dad slumped down on the one chair in the room. Suddenly he looked sad and old. I hadn't noticed how all this was wearing on him. It must be hard to know there wasn't anything he could do to bring Mom back since he couldn't time travel. He had to rely on me.

"I'll help her, Dad. I promise. I'll make the change she wants." I hoped that was a promise I could keep.

"I know you will, sweetie." Dad offered a limp smile, not at all convincing. "I'm just worried, that's all. It's not safe, not with that Watcher after her. I don't care about her changing the future, I just want her to be part of our present."

The Watcher had chased Mom through the centuries, threatening her if she kept on breaking time travel Rules, especially Rule Number One: Don't Do Anything to Change Events. Time travelers were only supposed to observe, and the Watcher had made it clear she'd do whatever she could to stop Mom. I'd seen what limits

she'd go to. She was behind two deaths that I knew of – Emile Zola in Paris and Giordano Bruno in Rome. I didn't want Mom to be a third.

"It's not like I ever get to talk to Mom," I reminded Dad. "She sends me messages, like this one. I don't even know how to get messages back to her." I'd caught glimpses of her, but she never let me get close. Mom was fine with breaking Rule Number One of time travel, but she kept all the other Rules, including the one where family members shouldn't time travel together. But the reason for that Rule was that it made the risk of changing the future greater, and since Mom actually wanted to change our future, she should have been all for it.

Except she had her own rules, and protecting us any way she could was her personal Rule Number One. She wasn't a cuddly, soft kind of mom, more like a mother bear. Even before I learned she could time travel, I knew she was different from other moms.

She didn't like to shop for clothes and go for mani-pedis like my best friend Claire's mom. She didn't bake cookies and cakes like Grandma did. Instead, she read constantly. You could ask her anything, from who invented the pink eraser on top of pencils to how long it took to build the Golden Gate Bridge, and she'd know the answer. She didn't waste time with small talk because, really, what was the point? I liked that about her.

So I wasn't surprised that her postcard wasn't full of flowery sentiment, just directions. Before where, though, was when. I hoped not during the great plague in the 1600s or Dickensian London when everything was so grimy and poor.

I've always considered Malcolm the history expert in our family, but there is one area of history I've read a lot about myself – English. English Renaissance to be exact, as in Henry VIII and Elizabeth I and Bloody Mary and the great English Armada fighting against the Spanish. I knew the rhyme about Henry VIII's six wives – divorced, beheaded, died, divorced, beheaded, survived. Meaning those were their fates – he really went through wives, even killing two of them for treason (those are the beheaded ones. The died one died in childbirth, that was Jane Seymour). Last year, Claire and I went to the Renaissance Faire dressed as ladies in waiting to Anne Boleyn (the first beheaded wife, the mother of Queen Elizabeth I).

I could manage to fit into that time period. It might even be fun, despite not having toilets. Plus, I'd have something really interesting to tell Claire – if Dad ever allowed me to talk about these things. Up to now, I'd just sent her messages about the places we'd seen, nothing about time travel, of course. And in exchange, she'd kept me up to date on

the latest stuff happening at home. Which wasn't a lot since most of our friends were away at camp, or worse, summer school. Traveling around Europe was definitely better than that!

"What's the best time to go to London?" I asked.

"You mean in terms of history?" Dad asked. "Or in terms of the weather? Because if you mean weather, there's no good time."

"But there's a clear worst time, right? Like the middle of winter – that's got to be the most depressing season, with all that famous pea-soup fog." Malcolm wrapped his arms around his chest as if he could feel the chill all the way here in Roman summer. "If I could choose any time, I'd pick spring during the rule of Elizabeth I. You could meet Shakespeare! Plus, that's when England was super powerful." That was exactly what I was hoping.

"If you want power, then you'd pick Queen Victoria," Dad said. "Under her rule, the sun never set on the British Empire because their colonies were everywhere, from North America to the Caribbean, from Africa to Asia."

"I suppose, but that seems like a pretty stuffy era." I was still rooting for Tudor England.

"There's no point in speculating." Dad shook his head. "You don't pick either the time or the place. Mom does that. Let's pack our stuff so we can leave as soon as I get a cheap flight to London. I'm sure I can find one for tomorrow on one of those discount airlines."

"We don't need to guess what time period," said Malcolm. "While Dad figures out flights, I'll go to an Internet café. Bet you I can figure out what Room 40 means and when you'll be in London."

That wasn't a bet worth taking. In fact, any bet with Malcolm about historical research would be like throwing your money away. He was that good.

The next morning we were crammed onto one of those flights to London that was so cheap, there were ads plastered all over the seats. Plus you had to pay for water. Good thing it was such a short hop, since I felt like we were on a winged bus more than an airplane. I half expected to see a row of passengers standing at the back, holding onto straps like on the subway.

"So what did you find out, Malcolm?" I asked once we were settled into our narrow seats. We'd been in such a rush to make the flight, there'd been no chance to talk about where we were going and why. "Something big from the look on your face."

"Yes!" Malcolm beamed. "You are SO lucky!"

"Meaning I'll get to meet Queen Elizabeth?"

"Much better than that! Room 40 in London can mean only one thing." Malcolm paused dramatically.

"Are you going to make me beg?"

"Come on, Malcolm," Dad urged. "Spill!"

"Okay, okay." My brother leaned forward eagerly. "Room 40 was where the cryptographers worked during World War I, where they cracked the codes used in German military and diplomatic messages."

"World War I?" My stomach dipped. How was that lucky? That was when millions of men died in brutal trench warfare, when poison gas was invented and first used on troops, when there was so much senseless slaughter, it was supposed to be the war to end all wars. Which, of course, it wasn't.

"Yes!" Malcolm didn't sound the least bit worried. But then, he wasn't the one about to be whisked away to a war zone. "Room 40 was the heart of British code cracking. They were able to read all the messages to and from German submarines, all their diplomatic dispatches, including the famous Zimmermann Telegram. I think that's why Mom wants you there – you need to help get the Zimmermann Telegram to the United States somehow. Maybe you're the one who intercepts it! Maybe you get to spy on Zimmermann himself!"

"The Zimmermann Telegram? Wasn't that the reason President Wilson finally declared war on Germany? So the Americans obviously got it, and Mira doesn't need to do anything." Dad had heard of this supposedly famous telegram, but I had no idea what either of them was talking about.

"First explain to me what this telegram is, okay?" I demanded, ignoring the flight attendant who was offering to sell us beer, wine, soda, duty-free perfume, chocolate, bus tickets, or an array of chips – I mean "crisps" – with flavors like kippers and beef pie. Ugh!

"Zimmermann was the German foreign minister. He sent a telegram to the German ambassador in Mexico telling him to offer the Mexican government arms and military aid if they would start  a war against the United States." Malcolm answered before Dad could say anything. "He promised that with Germany's help, Mexico could get back the –" And here Malcolm made air quotes. "– 'Territories' of New Mexico, Arizona, and Texas. Conniving, no? Germany wanted President Wilson to be so busy with his own troubles, he wouldn't enter World War I and save the Allies."

"That's despicable!"

"You got to admit, it was clever. But the British had been able to crack German codes for almost the whole war, thanks to some enemy codebooks that they had intercepted. So they deciphered the telegram quickly. The problem was, they had to figure out a way to get it into American hands without our government thinking it was forged propaganda to provoke America into entering the war. It took almost a month to get what they needed to prove the telegram was real. If you're not supposed to intercept the telegram yourself, then I'm betting you need to help the code crackers find that proof quicker, so we enter the war sooner."

"That's a big supposition," Dad said.

"Dad, we just studied this in AP United States history! It was so infuriating that Wilson refused to enter the war even after German submarines torpedoed ships traveling to and from America. Even though Americans on board were killed." My Berkeley peacenik brother sounded surprisingly like a vigilante warmonger.

"Just because you wish we'd declared war against Germany sooner doesn't mean that's the change Mom wants – or needs," Dad said, which was just what I was thinking.

"Well, why did she say Room 40 then? Like I said, that's the code-cracking room!"

"I believe you, and I've heard of the Zimmermann Telegram. I'm just not sure about your interpretation."

I wasn't sure either, but it seemed like a place to start. "What else can you tell me about Room 40? Do you know who any of the code crackers were?"

"I can tell you who cracked the Zimmermann Telegram –

Nigel de Grey!"

"That sounds like a fake name, if ever I've heard one." I rolled my eyes.

"It's real!" Malcolm said hotly. "And I can tell you something else about him. His day job, before he signed up for the war effort, was at a publisher's. He worked at William Heinemann's. So if you can't figure out a way into Room 40, try his old office at Heinemann's."

"Impressive, Malcolm." I wasn't being sarcastic. I was always amazed by how quickly he could track down information. He knew how to think inside, outside, under, and above the box. "You'd be a good spy yourself."

"Malcolm's Intelligence with a capital I," Dad agreed, unfolding the map of London he'd bought before we left Rome. "Here," he said, circling a spot on the map, "is our hotel. Here's the Admiralty Building, where Room 40 was. South of Trafalgar Square. Now it's the Ministry of Defense. And the publisher?" He looked at Malcolm, waiting.

"Covent Garden." Of course Malcolm knew. He bent over the map and pointed to a rose-colored splotch, just north of the river that ran through the city. The two points didn't seem far apart, maybe one subway stop.

"Since you know so much, can you reassure me that World War I London will be safe? The trenches were in France, right?" It seemed like I was the only one worried about me going into a war zone.

"You should be fine." Dad gave me an awkward, one-arm hug from his cramped seat. "The fighting happened in France, Belgium, and Russia."

"And Turkey, Palestine, Poland, Serbia, the Caucasus, Italy, Mesopotamia or the Ottoman Empire, whatever you want to call it, and, oh yeah, Africa. It was a world war, remember?" Malcolm raised his eyebrows dramatically. "But England was mostly okay. There were bombing raids, but nothing major."

"What's a little bomb every now and then?" I snorted.

"If it were really dangerous, your mother wouldn't ask you to go," Dad insisted.

There were two things wrong with that statement. First, when Dad said "your mother" instead of "mom," you knew you were in trouble. The second was that Mom seemed to have a different notion of risk than I did. She didn't worry about sending me to sixteenth-century Rome when there were all kinds of horrible diseases and everyday random violence. But if I asked to take BART to San Francisco by myself, I'd have to suffer a long lecture about the perils of public transit.

"Come on, Mira," Malcolm said. "The food will be the most dangerous thing there! You'll have to eat things like kidney pie and spotted dick. Ugh!"

Sometimes he could be so annoying. Especially when he was right. "You'll be facing the same hazards, then, eating

English food."

"Nope, not me," Malcolm gloated. "In the glorious present, there's lots of great food in London – Indian, Italian, Greek, probably even Californian. And, of course, McBurgers. But back in the day, it was all bubble and squeak, pasties, and bangers and mash."

"Those sound like cleaning products, not food!" I wished the airline would give out peanuts so I could shove some in my pockets. If my notebook could time travel with me, maybe a few snacks could too. But then, Mom had given me the notebook and pen, so maybe that's why I could take them with me – some special time travel-proof gimmick that peanuts wouldn't have.

"Really, Mira, you're worried about what you'll eat? Mom's counting on you! That's much more important."

Dad was right, of course. And we'd gotten way off track. The plane was already landing and we still hadn't figured out what my plan should be.

"How can I possibly get into Room 40 when it's a top secret military place doing top secret war stuff?"

"I know!" Malcolm's eyebrows shot up again. "You can borrow a page from the French playbook, from what you learned the first time you time traveled! Remember how the French military found the incriminating paper that showed them there was a French army officer selling secrets to the Germans?"

"Of course, the cleaning woman!" I almost could forgive him for the stupid food comments. "She was really an agent for the

French, but she worked in the German embassy and she found the treacherous note in the trash can. Not very smart of the Germans."

"Well, of course they didn't think their cleaning woman was a spy. Can't blame them for that. Anyway, that's how you can get into Room 40 – get a job as a cleaner."

"That's a good idea," Dad agreed. "But how can she be sure she'll be hired?"

"She has to try. After all, with most of the men away fighting the war, girls and women took all sorts of jobs," Malcolm explained. "There was a big labor shortage and that should work in her favor. If it doesn't, we'll think of something else."

"I guess that's better than nothing." I braced myself for the landing and took a deep breath. "At least for once I'll have an idea of where to go once I go into the past. That's something."

"Welcome to the United Kingdom!" the customs agent said as she stamped my passport. At least, I thought that was what she'd said. I'd been so busy worrying about the terrible cooking, I'd forgotten I'd have to decode British accents. Sometimes when Mom watched one of her BBC programs, I'd ask her to include the subtitles so I could understand the dialogue. Somehow the words sounded slanted to me, like people were speaking in italics, all jumbled together into total babble. At least the signs didn't have

strange accents, and we found our way easily onto the train to Victoria Station in central London.

It was exciting to go to a new city, to explore a new place, and I hoped we'd have time to see London before I was whirled away by a Touchstone. I could try not touching anything, but so far I hadn't been able to resist their magnetic pull.

"What do you want to see while we're here?" I asked Malcolm.

"The Tower of London," he answered without hesitation. "And of course, the British Museum, the National Gallery, Westminster Abbey. Oh, and London Bridge, though it's completely rebuilt. Maybe even the Sherlock Holmes Museum at the real 221B Baker Street. It might be too touristy and hokey, but it could still be fun."

"I'm thinking the Houses of Parliament or Big Ben could be the Wonder for my book. Or maybe Saint Paul's Cathedral." Dad was poring over tour guides as usual, planning what he needed to take photos of for the book he was making on the Modern Wonders of the World. That was his excuse to our friends when we left. After all, he couldn't tell the truth, that we were following our time traveling mom through time and space. And the Modern Wonders was a pretty convenient explanation, since every city we'd been to so far had something distinctive that could qualify as a Wonder. Lucky for him. What if Mom had sent a postcard from Iowa or Bratislava or Outer Mongolia? Or Inner Mongolia, for that matter.

As the train pulled into Victoria Station, I couldn't help but think of the Harry Potter books. Okay, this wasn't King's Cross

Station, where Harry would take the train to Hogwarts, but it was pretty close.

I may have been embarrassed to make the Harry Potter comparison, but not Malcolm. "Let's look for track nine and three-quarters! I bet they have a sign here now for Harry Potter fans."

"Wrong station, Malcolm. London is huge and there are a bunch of different train stations."

"But isn't this the main one, the most important one?"

"Maybe, but it's not the Harry Potter one." For once I could be the nerdy expert. "That's King's Cross, and maybe there's a marker there."

Dad looked up from the guidebook, grinning. "There is! You can see a blank wall labeled 'Platform 9 ¾' with a luggage trolley in front of it in case you want to smash it into the wall."

"We should go there, Dad!" Malcolm begged. "Not as tourists, but I bet you that's a Touchstone. How could it not be?" I forgot that he had dressed up as Harry Potter one Halloween. Now all his Potter-mania was coming back, fullforce.

"Wrong story, Malcolm." I shook my head. "We'll find a

Touchstone, believe me. It doesn't have to be that one."

The inside of the station was disappointingly un-magical, not rich in Touchstones at all. It didn't even have an exotic foreign glow since all the signs were in English. We could have been in New York or Washington, DC. Until we stepped outside and one of those classic red double-decker British buses rumbled by, followed by taxis that were big, black, and snub-nosed, more like hearses than cabs. But the most foreign part was that at first glance, it looked like nobody was driving because the driver's seat was empty. Except of course, the driver didn't sit on the left side in England. The steering wheel was on the other side, and all the cars and buses were driving on the wrong side of the road.

Other than that, London struck me as a lot like any big American city. There was a rush of energy and noise like you feel in New York, people walking quickly, talking  on phones, texting, the usual urban scene. It was silly, but I was disappointed. I knew not to expect a Harry Potter world, but I wanted London to feel different, more historical. Maybe once we got away from the train station, it would.

Across the street stood a statue of a man on horseback, raised high on a pedestal. That promised a glimpse into history. The

monument could even be a Touchstone.

"How about that?" I asked Malcolm. "What do you think?"

"Look carefully before you cross," Dad warned. "We're used to traffic coming from the other direction. He was right – it was disorienting to have the cars on the wrong side, I mean the left side. What were the British trying to prove by that, anyway? We dodged our way across, protected by the crowds heading to and from the station. On the other side of the road, the area around the statue was oddly empty. Nobody paused to look at it. Everyone was in too much of a hurry to get wherever they were going. We must have seemed like hick tourists, like the people who take pictures of the fake Michelangelo's David outside in the Piazza della Signoria, not realizing the real statue is inside, protected from the elements. But this was a real sculpture, not a copy. I could feel the truthfulness of it, the years radiating from it.

"Good pick!" said Malcolm as he read the label on the monument. "The first thing you see coming out of the station is this, a statue of Marshal Ferdinand Foch!"

I'd never heard of Ferdinand Foch, but I knew my brother would explain things to me. I wouldn't even need to ask.

"He was France's most famous general," Malcolm continued, right on cue. "And the leader of the Allies in World War I. Of the whole Allied army, not just France. The British gave him the rank of field marshal under the Order of England. That's why he's here, in London, and that's why they put this quote of his on the base."

I read the words on the pedestal, "I am conscious of having served England as I served my country." Not exactly poetic or fiery with inspiration, but I got the distinctly British point. A pulsing shimmer rose from the inscription, cloaking the statue in a golden haze. How weird! Was I learning to see Touchstones, to recognize them before I touched them?

"So, I'm off to World War I London?" It wasn't really a question. There was no point in waiting, though I'd hoped for at least a glimpse of Big Ben. The statue had made up my mind for me. I waved good-bye to Dad and Malcolm, then reached out to touch the words.

"Wait, Mira!" Dad grabbed my arm. "Are you sure you're ready? Do you know what you're going to do?"

I nodded firmly. "Room 40, the Admiralty Building. I'll get some kind of job as a cleaner and figure things out from there. Don't worry, I can survive on cucumber sandwiches."

"Don't you want to see London with us first?" Dad actually

looked teary eyed. Was there something else I should be worried about? Something besides terrible food, hard-to-understand accents, and the occasional bomb?

"It's more important to help Mom." There was plenty of time for sightseeing after she was safely home with us.

"Anyway, not every statue is a Touchstone," Malcolm remarked. "What makes you sure this one is?"

It was weird. I'd found Touchstones before almost by accident — okay, entirely by accident, though I'd made some good guesses. But I knew this statue was one. I could see purple-blue waves throbbing from it now, a kind of temporal halo.

"I can tell," I said. "I'm getting better at this time travel stuff, just like Mom said I would. And this time I won't disappear on you guys. We can actually say good-bye."

Dad hugged me tightly. "You're right, of course. Good-bye and good luck!"

"Ta-ta, cheerio, and pip-pip!" Malcolm saluted.

"See you soon, I hope!" I gave my brother a quick hug, then reached out and touched the plaque on the base. Lights crackled around me and I felt the familiar dizzying whirl, the whooshing of sun, moon, stars, and comets. I wished I would find myself in Diagon Alley, surrounded by witches and wizards, maybe a gnome or two, but I knew better.

?

When the ground stopped teetering and I could look around, nothing seemed magical at all. The day was gray and cold. I found myself in a busy street lined with crumbling brick buildings, shabby tenements with darkened windows. Dingy laundry hung in lines across the narrow alleyways. This may have been historical London, but there was nothing charming here. Just three-story houses of shuddering poverty with narrow doors and small pinched windows, as if even sunlight cost money. The whole place was dank, muddy, broken-down, stinking of fish and rot and some indefinable yuck. The stench was so thick it had a physical presence, like a filthy hand pressed against my nose.

A small girl dressed in tatters scrubbed clothes in a metal tub while her even smaller brother smeared the dirt on a nearby window with a filthy rag. Children just as poorly dressed, barefoot and coatless in the chill, ran around, shouting shrilly. Surly women shouldered their way through the crowds, baskets and babies balanced on their hips. This was a poor neighborhood, the misery of life filling the air with its own rancid smell. It reminded me of the photos I'd seen of New York slums at the turn of the century, places where families slept ten to a room.

I looked at my own clothes. A plain deep-green dress with a neat collar and cuffs, a felt hat on my head that wasn't fancy, but not torn or dirty either. My curly dark  hair was held back from my face with clips, then fell loosely to my shoulders. Most important, I had a thick dark cloak to ward off the seeping cold. Plus I was wearing shoes. Ordinary clothes that were extraordinary in this place So I didn't belong with the poor, which was a huge relief, and I hurried through the maze of streets, past carts loaded with potatoes, wheelbarrows full of coal, baskets of cabbage, people buying and selling all sorts of goods, looking for a way out of the slum. Even the poorest places I'd seen in nineteenth-century Paris seemed luxurious in comparison to these miserable people.

My head felt itchy with imaginary lice and I was sure I'd caught some nasty disease from all the coughing, hacking, and spitting around me. Each street was filthier than the next until finally I came to a broad clearing, ringed by impressive buildings – a clothing store next to a bakery next to a bank, all clean and freshly painted, with broad doors and big plate glass windows. This was definitely a better neighborhood. I stopped to take a deep breath. It even smelled better here.

And it felt more modern. The streets were wide enough that cars whizzed by next to horse-drawn carriages. Double-decker buses with wooden slats for sides and truck-like fronts rumbled on the cobblestones next to strange steam-driven trucks. There was an odd mix on the streets. As many steam-driven wagons as gasoline-fueled buses as cars as carts as carriages. It was like some kind of primordial transportation stew, with all these creatures vying for survival. Some would be evolutionary winners while others would sink back into the muck.

There were street lamps, but no lane lines or traffic lights, so police officers directed the swirl of vehicles and people. It was so chaotic,  I couldn't tell which side of the road drivers were supposed to be on – cars seemed to come from all directions at once. Maybe that was all being decided by evolution too – left side over right or right side over left?

The better-dressed men wore black coats and top hats, the women long dresses and fancy hats. Not that different from what I'd seen in nineteenth-century Paris. Maybe a touch more modern, a touch less elegant. The poorer people wore aprons, muddy boots, and coarse clothes in grays and browns. But they all had shoes and weren't as scabbily miserable as those I'd seen before. The Touchstone must have sent me to the worst part of the city. It was a relief to be somewhere nicer.

Nicer, but noisier. A large crowd of people clustered together ahead of me – mostly women – all facing the same direction. Nobody stared at me or told me to leave, so I pushed my way through the knots of people murmuring and clapping every now and then until I could see what they were watching.

I was half hoping for a magician, a circus act, something fun to erase the vision of misery from the slums. Instead, a woman stood at the top of the steps leading up to a building that looked like a domineering government office. The woman herself looked just as formidable, maybe because while some people cheered and applauded, others jeered and hooted, yelling insults.

"Go back to your kitchen! Scrub them pots!" one man screeched.

"Women will vote when dogs can talk!" another bellowed.

"What man would want an ugly old maid like you?" screamed a man with a face like a crumpled piece of paper, not exactly a charmer himself.

The woman ignored the catcalls, her chin tilted up defiantly. Her clothes were simple, her face equally plain, but her voice was loud and clear.

"We must continue the fight until the battle is won!" she called, holding up her fist. "The long days and nights in jail, the hunger strikes, the brutal force feedings – none of this shall be in vain! Parliament asks women to work for the war. They ask us to put in long hours at factories, doing dangerous work for low pay. They ask us to nurse soldiers torn apart by bombardments. They ask us to sacrifice again and again. Yet still we aren't given a voice in our own government! Still we're denied the vote!"

Dad had taken me to a war protest once in San Francisco, but this was much more exciting. The energy surging through the crowd swept me up, and I surprised myself by yelling back with the other women around me.

"Votes for women! Votes for women!" At first I was hesitant, but as the women roared beside me, my faltering voice rose. This was something I believed in after all. Women should be allowed to vote!

"Votes for monkeys!" heckled a group of men, looking distinctly apish themselves.

"Votes for women!" we yelled back. Now my voice was strong and sure. I felt part of something big and important. When one woman faced the bullying men and shouted for them to leave, I joined her and several others, linking arms into a human chain to keep the men away.

"Don't pick a fight with a real man, sister!" snorted a red-faced man wearing a leather apron.

"Don't see any real men here!" the woman snapped and she shoved his beefy chest. I was afraid he'd haul off and hit her, but another man grabbed his arm and dragged him away, muttering about crazy witches.

"Don't bother with these cows. They're wasting their breath," one of the other hecklers said, hitching up his suspenders and stalking off with his angry friends. "Pigs will fly before women get the vote!"

As the rowdiest men left, the woman on the steps called out louder than ever, "To those who think a flying pig is more likely than a voting woman, I say this: be prepared to be amazed. Women will vote. And women will run for public office. And women will win!"

The crowd erupted in wild cheers. I yelled with them, my throat hoarse, my heart pounding with excitement. I wasn't from this time, I didn't belong, but I felt very much part of the moment as I pumped my fist and yelled, "Vote, vote, vote!" with everyone else. It was weird. I was part of this group in a way I'd never been before when I time traveled. Then I remembered the Watcher and how I was supposed to just observe, not participate. If she saw me, would she arrest me? For a second, I stopped chanting, searching the crowd for the Watcher's beautiful face, but I didn't see her. Anyway, if I only stood and watched, I'd look totally out of place. Better to be part of the crowd, to blend in. I joined the roar of voices lifting upward in an enormous plea for women's rights. I wasn't afraid anymore, but filled with the courage of all the women around me.

"And now to continue with our program today, I give you Mary Richardson," the speaker was saying now, presenting a tall, angular woman standing next to her.

"You may know me as the painting slasher, the woman who attacked Velasquez's Rokeby Venus in the National Gallery. I stood by that act then and I stand by it now. How can the government punish me for harming the image of a woman when every day, every single day in this 'civilized' nation, real women, flesh-and-blood women, are beaten by their husbands,

worked like animals by their bosses, treated like property by the law? I tried to destroy a picture of the most beautiful woman in mythological history as a protest against the government for destroying Mrs. Pankhurst, who is the most beautiful character in modern history. How many times must she be sent to prison for asserting women's rights before our voices are heard? Since our cries are ignored, we must act, for actions are harder to dismiss."

This woman had knifed a painting, a masterpiece by Velasquez? I'd been excited before, but now my stomach churned queasily. I dropped the hands of the protestors on either side of me, no longer part of the human chain. How did destroying art help the cause of women? Couldn't she have passed around a petition or held a protest march or something?

I must have looked as bad as I felt, because a round-faced woman with warm brown eyes and red hair piled puffily on her head held my elbow gently. She was the one who'd shoved the beefy man in the chest.

"Sister, you look like to faint. Those boorish churls haven't upset you, have they?"

"You were very brave!" I said. "I thought that man would punch you in the face."

"I'd have liked to see him try!" Her eyes glinted with laughter. "Besides, you looked ready to wallop him yourself!"

I stared at the ground, embarrassed. "He deserved it!"

"That's the spirit! Use that anger! It's what fuels our cause, what keeps us going – righteous indignation! Miss Mary Robinson, the woman speaking, now she's truly courageous. She's dared things I'd never try."

"You mean slashing the painting?" I frowned.

"Ah, you don't agree with her tactics." The woman sighed. I didn't want to disappoint her, but it seemed wrong to damage a work of art to make a point. I could hear Mary describing how she'd hidden the knife in the folds of her skirts as she walked into the gallery, how she'd paced around, waiting for the right moment to strike.

"You need to know something about Mary, then maybe you'll understand. She and a friend were protesting for women's rights at the races, at Epsom Downs. They tried to stop the races to get the men to listen to them. When nothing else worked, the two of them ran in front of the horses. The friend, Emily Davison, was crushed by a horse and died. Mary was chased and badly beaten by a raging mob."

Now I really felt sick. Women had died for this cause? I had no idea!

"Oh dear, I'm making things worse, aren't I?" the moon-faced woman said. "You're quite the sensitive soul." She guid-  ed me through the crowd to the steps near where the speakers stood and sat me down on the cold stone. "You rest here and I'll fetch you some water."

"I'm fine," I assured her, and really, I was, but the woman insisted. For a second, I wondered if she was a Watcher, trying to trap me. But her face was so kind and her worry seemed so genuine, I told myself I was being ridiculously paranoid. Still, when the first speaker left the stage to Mary and came down the steps to join us, I looked up at her nervously, as if she, too, hid a knife in her skirts.

"Sylvia, this is. . ." The brown-eyed woman paused. "I don't believe I know your name. This is Sylvia Pankhurst, the head of the Workers' Suffrage Federation. I'm Cecily Townsend."

"And I'm. . ." I hesitated. Who should I be? Obviously an American, since I'd never be able to carry off an accent like Cecily's. "I'm Miriam Lodge." There, that was simple enough.

"I see that you're from the United States," Sylvia observed, meaning that she heard it. "My mother was just there, speaking to women's groups in several cities. She admires your Miss Alice Paul and Miss Jane Addams. As do I, naturally. Though I admit, we British are puzzled by the sweet decorum of most American suffragists. I warrant there would be no defacing of paintings in the National Gallery in Washington."

"I should hope not," I blurted out, realizing too late it wasn't a very tactful thing to say.

"Funny, isn't it, that it's we 'prim' British who are using

violent means to call attention to our cause. Not because we enjoy breaking windows or setting businesses on fire, but because we have no choice. Without strong actions, our cause is lost, as Mary said. Men have ever rebelled violently when deprived of their rights, as you Americans so famously did at your Boston Tea Party. So why should women be any different?"

"I admire your bravery, but dumping tea is very different from damaging a great work of art. That doesn't help your cause and destroys something that belongs to everyone." I suppose I should have said nothing, just nodded politely, but I couldn't help myself, especially since she'd basically said that British women had more courage than American women. It was one thing to call me a coward, but not all American women!

"I admit it's an extreme measure." Sylvia pursed her lips as if she tasted something extra sour. "But we have been thrown into prison countless times for nothing more than bringing a petition to Parliament. We have been treated as common criminals, not as political prisoners, as are the Irish rebels – men – demanding their political rights. And when we go on hunger strikes to protest our miserable conditions, we are strapped into chairs, with tubes brutally thrust down our throats and force-fed, a cruel torture." Her voice trembled, and for a minute, I thought she'd burst into tears. Instead, she squared her shoulders. "It is the government who is violent toward us. How else can we respond?"

"I'm so sorry, that sounds awful. I didn't know." So mobs

beating up women protestors wasn't even the worst? What a horrible time period this was! If this was World War I England, like Malcolm thought, the war was only part of the nightmare. Maybe I was supposed to do something for women's rights, not the war effort? Could Room 40 have anything to do with women's suffrage?

"And yet my mother has been to your country, exposing precisely these practices." Sylvia sat down next to me as if we were on a park bench. On stage, Mary was still talking, now describing her arrest and trial, clearly a story Sylvia had heard many times already.

"Who is your mother?" I asked, though I probably hadn't heard of her. She'd already mentioned two American women who must have had something to do with suffrage, and I didn't know who they were. I'd have to remember to ask Malcolm to look up Alice Paul and Jane Addams once I got back home.

"Emmeline Pankhurst. She founded the WSPU, the Women's Social and Political Union."

Emmeline Pankhurst? That was the woman Mary Richardson had mentioned, the reason she'd hacked at the Velasquez painting.

"I'm sorry the government treated her so badly. What did they do?"

"Besides arresting her, throwing her into solitary confinement, force-feeding? You Americans are such innocents!"

She didn't mean innocent in a good way. The way she said it, it sounded more like stupid. "I'm sorry!" I sputtered. "I don't mean

to offend you, but our newspapers don't write about those details!"
Okay, I was guessing about that, but it seemed a safe assumption.

"Oh, of course they don't. I'm the one who should apologize." Sylvia's face softened and for a moment, she looked kind, gentle even. Then she pulled herself up, straightening her back. I could see a steeliness take hold of her, like the hardness she needed to face such an unjust world.

"Just for my mother, Parliament passed the Cat and Mouse Act. Force-feeding was so brutal, it gave Parliament bad press. Poor little lords, not wanting to tarnish their good names. Instead they decided to release women from prison if they grew too weak from fasting. Then once the women had regained their health, they'd be arrested once more, put in and out of prison at the whim of the Crown."

No wonder Sylvia was so angry, so bitter. It seemed like a cruel game for a government to play, toying with prisoners the way cats tease mice before finally killing them. I shuddered, thinking about the Watcher chasing after Mom.

"Is your mother okay?" I asked. "She must be very brave." Was Mom courageous? It didn't seem like the same thing, fighting for the rights of many people and trying to help only your family. Suddenly it all seemed small and selfish. I wondered if I'd suffer for something I believed in. I didn't think so. Was it worth being shoved in jail to win the right to vote? What would I be willing to go to prison for?

I thought about Giordano Bruno, in sixteenth-century Rome, willing to die for his scientific beliefs that the earth orbited the sun instead of the other way around. I thought of Emile Zola in nineteenth-century Paris, ready to face prison to right a brutal injustice. Each time I'd gone into the past, I'd met people with big ideas they were willing to fight for. Sylvia and her mother were the same. And so was Mary, even if I didn't agree with destroying art. She must have finished her speech now because a wave of applause thundered over us. More cheering, more chanting, as women started to leave. The meeting, the protest, whatever it was, was over.

I stood up, wiping dirt off my skirt, and offered a hand to Sylvia. She took it and pulled herself up. "Your mother?" I asked again.

"She is the strongest person I know," Sylvia said. "And the most noble. She's devoted her life to this cause and all her daughters, the three of us, have fought by her side. Until recently. The war changed that." I wondered if she'd been arrested herself, if the police were waiting to send her back to prison. Was she a mouse, hiding from the cat?

"Emmeline has chosen to support the government and the war effort. She thinks women should wait for more secure times before pushing for the vote," Sylvia continued, her voice sad and low. "I say we can't wait, and I disagree completely with the war.

Our mission is to end it as quickly as possible and in the meanwhile to support all conscientious objectors and universal suffrage, votes for unpropertied men and all women." She looked at me pointedly, as if asking me to choose sides.

I really didn't know who was right. "That must be hard, disagreeing with your mother. Especially when you admire her so much."

Sylvia nodded. "It's been the cruelest thing to happen to me, far more painful than prison. It's easy to gird yourself against your enemies, it's far harder to do that with the people you love and trust the most."

"This will help," Cecily said, returning with a glass of water. I'd been so caught up with Sylvia, I hadn't even noticed she'd left. "You look like you could use some yourself, Sylvia. Are you alright?"

I was relieved for a reason to hand the water straight to Sylvia. It was so brown and cloudy, I could almost see cholera and typhoid swimming in its murkiness.

"Yes, yes, fine." Sylvia took the glass and drank a muddy sip. "I was just explaining to Miss Lodge how my mother and I have parted over philosophical differences. It's a fatiguing memory."

"I should say so! You know how much I respect your mother and your older sister, Christabel, but it's hard to forgive them for pushing you out of the movement you fought so hard for!" Cecily seemed angrier about the rift than Sylvia.

"It's their movement now, what's left of it. We've made our own, and perhaps after the war, we'll join forces once again," Sylvia said, sounding like she didn't believe it herself.

Cecily certainly didn't. She looked liked she'd swallowed a bug as she took the empty glass. If she'd sipped from the glass, she might have. "I'll walk you to your rooms, Miss Lodge, make sure you get back safely."

"That's very kind of you, but there's no need to bother," I said. What was the story behind that sour face? For a second I wondered if I should take her up on the offer so I could ask her what really happened between mother and daughter. But I couldn't let gossip distract me.

Anyway, the only place I knew to go was the mysterious Room 40. "Actually, I was heading for the Admiralty Building, if you could kindly point me in the right direction."

"The Admiralty Building?" Cecily asked. "Why ever are you going there?"

I bit my lip, thinking. Why didn't I come up with plausible stories before I said anything? Of course she'd ask me that and now I had to quickly invent an excuse.

"Um, well, my cousin works there and he's supposed to help me find a place to stay." Was that probable? There wouldn't be a way to check all the employees – my cousin could be anyone. I'd call him Morton Wallrod after Mom's time traveling friend. His name really was Morton and he looked like a walrus with his puffy cheeks and bushy mustache taking up most of his face.

"You mean to say you have no lodgings?" Sylvia asked.

"Not yet, but I will. I'm sure my cousin has found a suitable room." I tried to sound as proper as I could. "Suitable room" sounded good, like I knew what I was doing.

"I don't mean to pry," Cecily said, lowering her voice to a whisper as if she were a spy about to divulge a secret, "but do you have the necessary funds? I only ask because we help women like you. It's one of the things our group is known for."

Well, that was lucky, since I didn't have any money and I had no idea where I'd end up spending the night. I'd pictured myself sleeping on a stiff wooden pew in a freezing-cold church, the only place I thought might be open all night.

Sylvia touched my arm gently. "There's no shame in poverty. If you haven't a place to stay, I can help you. We often see women who have run away from abusive homes, and we do all we can for them. And you're an American, so if you've run away, you've come a very long way indeed."

Was that a good cover story? Should I say that was exactly what had happened, that I'd used up my meager savings to pay for steamship passage to London, hoping to find a long lost cousin? That I was fleeing a cruel father? I hated to say anything mean about Dad, but I wouldn't really be talking about him. I had a split second to decide all this, and since I couldn't come up with anything better and I did need a place to stay, I smiled weakly at Sylvia and nodded.

"You're right, that's just what I've done. I'm trying to find my aunt, but I don't have an address for her. All I know is that her son works at the Admiralty Building." I admired how neatly I'd paired my two lies together – they fit so nicely! "I just had to leave, and they're the only family I have, though my aunt and my father haven't spoken for ages."

Sylvia looked satisfied, like she'd guessed a riddle correctly and was congratulating herself on how clever she'd been. "We've solved tougher problems, I assure you. We'll find your cousin and aunt, but for now you can stay with my mother." After what she'd said about their disagreement, I was surprised. "We've chosen different paths, but we're still a family. Besides, though we may disagree, Emmeline has no reason to argue with you. She often takes in women in need. In fact it's something she takes pride in." Sylvia took a slender metal case out of the purse strung around her wrist and opened it to reveal a stack of cream-colored, engraved business cards. "This is my address and this is my mother's." She wrote on the back of one of the cards with an elegant fountain pen, also stashed in the purse. "Show Emmeline this card and she'll know I sent you."

I took the card gratefully, though I wondered how the mother would feel about her daughter offering her home as a refuge to a complete stranger. Would I really be welcome there?

"I'd take you there myself," Sylvia went on. "But I need to go to a meeting now with Mary. Can you find your way?"

"I'm sure I can." Though I wasn't at all certain. "Thank you, thank you so much," I said, as Sylvia and Cecily turned to go. I'd only just met them, but I felt close to them. Maybe because we'd faced the rude men together, maybe because they'd been so kind to me. Whatever the reason, they gave me a strange sense of warmth, of belonging, that I hadn't felt before when I'd been in the past.

Without them, I felt starkly alone. I was tempted to go straight to the house, to continue the connection with the suffragists, but Mom had been clear about Room 40. I still needed directions, so I walked into a nearby chemist's shop to ask my way.

"Mira!" a man's voice called as the door shut behind me. Mira? Who knew my name here? There was only one possible person, Morton, or the Walrus Man, the namesake of my invented cousin. I turned back through the door and sure enough, there he was, looking as much like a walrus as ever with his thick brush of a

 mustache and wobbly jowls.

I'd met Morton when I first traveled through time. Mom had sent him to guide me on the missions she'd planned for me, first in Paris and again in Rome. And now here in London. He wasn't exactly my friend, but I was glad to see him.

Morton dabbed at his glistening forehead with a large handkerchief. It was freezing cold out, so it wasn't the temperature that was making him sweat. Was the Watcher following him?

"Morton! I wondered if I'd find you here. Have you seen the Watcher? Is she already after Mom?"

Morton shook his head. "Not yet, but she will be, you can count on it."

"Where's Mom now? Can I get a note to her?" I didn't know what I'd say, but I wanted some kind of contact with her. Usually that was the only thing Morton could really do for me – be the go-between with Mom.

"She's working on this from her end, in the household of the prime minister, David Lloyd George. It's hard for her to leave, so she warned me she can't get notes to you this time. I'm to give you instructions and she'll take care of the rest." This wasn't the usually vague "she's somewhere" excuse – Morton was telling me exactly where Mom was!

"Could I go see her there? Or leave her a message?"

Morton snorted. "You know better than that, Mira! Look, I'm telling you this because she said to. She's trusting you won't put her – or yourself – in danger by getting too close. Don't worry about her. She's safer from the Watcher there than anywhere else."

So Mom was worried about the Watcher too. Somehow that made me more afraid, not less.

"I'm sorry your mother is asking you to do these things. While she's in a comfortable mansion, you're on the streets. She's taking risks, of course, but so are you! I keep telling her that you're just a child. And time travel is far too complicated for you to understand. She should leave you out of it entirely."

I was fourteen, not some little kid. Maybe I hadn't done well enough before, but I'd get things right this time.

"I'm getting better at this, really I am!" I bristled. "I recognized a Touchstone before I even touched it, and that's a definite improvement. Tell me what Mom needs. What should I do in Room 40?"

"Let's walk while we talk," Morton said, taking my elbow and guiding me along the street. "I always feel like a sitting duck, standing in the open this way. Better to keep moving."

"But you said you hadn't seen the Watcher."

"I said not yet – I don't want to take any chances."

We dodged our way across the broad street between cars and carts, taking advantage of the clearing made by the police escorting a group of men wearing strange white collars and bandages. I still didn't know the exact date, but the British bobbies wore the same helmet hat as in modern day London.

"Are they transporting prisoners to a hospital?" I asked.

"Those aren't convicts!" Morton sounded outraged. "They're soldiers who were wounded in the war. They wear those collars so people will know the sacrifices they've made and accord them the respect they deserve. Prisoners indeed!"

"Which war? What date is it? The policemen almost look

modern, but this isn't twenty-first-century London, that's for sure."

Malcolm assumed this trip was about World War I, but England had been in a lot of wars. When had they fought in India? In Burma? In South Africa? Wasn't that one of the problems with having such a huge empire, there was always a war going on somewhere?

"Today is January sixteenth, 1917 and the war is the Great War, World War I."

Okay, Malcolm was right. Big surprise. And Mom wanted me to do something that would change the course of the war. That seemed like way too big a change to make, way too risky. I was still hoping this was all about votes for women. If only Room 40 was where the suffragists held their meetings!

"So what are my directions?" I pressed. "What happens today that's so important?"

Morton leaned closer to me as we turned up a narrow side street. He lowered his voice. "Something crucial. Today, Room 40 intercepts the Zimmermann Telegram."

A shiver ran through me. Malcolm was right again!

"Do you really want to do this?" Morton asked. "We can find you a Touchstone, send you back to the right time. I know about Rome, how you ended up in prison, how you were almost sent to the galleys. Your mother rescued you then, but she won't be able to this time. You're really on your own."

"No!" I insisted. "I'm here and I'll do my job. This time will be easier, because Mom's telling me so much more. I'm not guessing blindly, right? You'll tell me what I'm supposed to do?"

We were walking through a park now, near the river, and as the road curved, a familiar shape loomed ahead. I stopped, staring. It was Big Ben. My first memory of it probably came from the Peter Pan movie, when Peter and all the kids fly around it before soaring off to Neverland. Here it was, in real life, with the Houses of Parliament spread behind it. Now I felt like I was in London.

"Come on!" Morton nudged me. "Let's keep moving."

My eyes fixed on the tower, I followed slowly. It was so stately, so magnificent, and so quintessentially British. On the broad river below, small boats skimmed through its reflection, next to big flatboats heaped high with hay. The shore was lined with wooden huts, but from this distance I couldn't tell if they were stores, warehouses, or beach cabanas. They certainly looked makeshift, like a wolf could huff and puff and blow them all down.

"Listen, Mira, this time I'll be specific, very specific." Morton's voice was low and urgent.

I tore my eyes off of Big Ben and the whirl of boats in its shadow, facing

Mom's friend. I held my breath, waiting. No more guesswork! Mom had already been more detailed than ever before when she named Room 40 and now this.

"You see that man waiting by the corner over there?" Morton pointed to a tall figure with a neatly trimmed mustache wearing a bowler hat and a long, flapping black coat. He carried a briefcase in one hand, a cane in the other. "That's Heinrich Albert, a German spy. Your mother thinks his briefcase contains incriminating proof of Germany's efforts to start a Mexican-American war. You need to follow him, get the case from him somehow, and deliver it to Room 40. It's what they need to show the Americans that the Zimmermann Telegram isn't a forgery, that the threat from Germany is all too real."

"I can't just steal his briefcase!" My heart beat so quickly, I felt like throwing up. Who did Mom think I was, James Bond or something?

"Nothing so obvious, of course!" the Walrus hissed. "Distract him or wait until he's looking at something else, then snatch the briefcase and get away. Or talk the man himself into coming with you to Room 40. Tell him his long-lost girlfriend is waiting for him there. Or drug him with a sleeping pill.  Do whatever ridiculous thing is necessary! All I know is what your mother said – she told me Albert would be waiting on the corner with the briefcase and that you need to get the case to Room 40."

"If it's so easy, then you do it!" I squawked. I wished Malcolm was with me. He'd been right about everything! He'd know how to handle the spy.

"I've already done far more than I should have!" Morton scowled. "I keep telling your mother, this is crazy! It's too risky! She has to stop! But does she listen?" Morton mopped his sweaty forehead again. "This is the last time, the last time, I'm telling you. Steal the briefcase, don't steal it. I don't care!" He turned and quickly vanished in the crowded street behind us.

Which left me alone with a German spy, a briefcase of evil papers, and a Watcher possibly looming around the corner, ready to snatch me and Mom. Which of Morton's hare-brained ideas was best? Could I come up with anything better? What would Malcolm do?

I walked up to the man, palms both sweaty and ice-cold at once. A women with a nurse's cap, the kind you see in old movies, joined him, and then an old couple arrived, nobody talking to each other, all just standing in front of a bookstore. There had to be a reason they were all there. Could such an odd assortment of people be a group of spies? I stepped back, unsure how close I could safely get.

If I were a beautiful woman, like the Watcher, I could bat my violet eyes at the man, ask for the time or a cigarette, like in an old movie, and easily distract him. But I was just a girl. Should I stomp on his foot like a crazy person and snatch the briefcase while he hopped around in pain? Would the nurse grab me then? Surely the old couple couldn't do anything. Maybe I should I act like a frightened, lost child and beg for his help, then run off with the case when he wasn't looking? Why didn't Morton give me more time to plan things? Sure, this time he'd been clear about what I needed to do, but I felt like I'd been thrown into the deep end and was struggling to keep my head above water.

As I worked up the nerve to do something, anything, a double-decker bus with wood-paneled sides and an open top rumbled up to the curb. That's why they were all there – this was a bus stop! The man climbed on and I quickly followed, going up the winding stairs in back to the upper level, sitting on the bench behind him.

I let out the breath I'd been holding. Now I had some time to figure out what to do. Bus rides, in my experience, were long ordeals. Nobody took the bus for fewer than fifteen minutes, and a half hour was more likely. Still, it would be safer to do something sooner, just in case. I studied the back of the man's head, noticing the hairs springing from his ears, the square set of his shoulders, the stiff way he sat. Was he really a spy? He looked like he could be anybody, a dentist or an insurance salesman. The briefcase was on the floor by the man. It too looked totally ordinary. Leather, with creases showing its age. No lock, nothing to make it seem top secret. Maybe I could reach under the seat and grab it without him noticing. I nudged the

case with my foot as the bus turned a corner. Now it was against the side of the bus. If we went uphill, it would slide back to me all by itself. This whole thing could turn out to be easier than I thought.

I allowed myself a minute to admire the view, impressive from so high up. To the right, the river Thames flowed, dotted with all the boats I'd seen before. The dome of St. Paul's cathedral loomed ahead, taller than the surrounding build-ings, like St. Peter's in Rome. Was the man busy admiring the land-scape? All I could tell was that he was looking straight ahead, his back rigid. He didn't seem relaxed enough to be enjoying the view.

I bent down and tugged gently at the briefcase, sliding it further from the man, closer to me. The bus stopped and more pas-sengers clambered aboard. A heavy-set woman wheezed as she sat next to me, setting baskets of groceries on the floor. Between her bulk and that of her baggage, any quick exit was blocked now. Should I change seats? But then I wouldn't be as close to the briefcase. I could touch it with the tips of

my shoes.

Then I had one of those lightbulb moments that happen often in cartoons, but rarely in real life.

As the bus slowed to its next stop, I got up quickly, catching my foot on one of the baskets, tipping it over so that cabbages, potatoes, carrots, onions, a cacophony of vegetables, bounced along the floor.

"Blimey, me shopping!" the woman howled, racing to catch the escaping vegetables. As she shoved the German spy to grab

some potatoes, I snatched the briefcase, ran down the staircase and out of the bus, dashing down the narrowest, busiest street I could see. A commotion erupted behind me, a shrill whistle and a voice howling, "Thief! Stop that girl!"

My heart pounded as I pushed my way past tradesmen carrying pipes and a worker with a ladder. Bad luck, I thought as I dodged between carts and wheelbarrows, the briefcase held tight to my chest.

My skirts were heavy and dragged in the mud, but I didn't dare slow down. I ran so hard, my breath was ragged, echoing in my ears. Had I done this? Had I really stolen a spy's papers? I couldn't stop and think, just kept on running.

There was no more yelling. No sounds of anyone chasing me, and still I ran for a good ten minutes. The houses around me now were small brick buildings, tucked behind cobbled streets and sidewalks. There was no sign of the spy. No sign of anyone after me. I slowed to a walk, catching my breath, clutching the briefcase tightly. It was quieter here, away from the bustle of stores and factories. And cleaner too. One woman swept the pavement in front of her house. Another washed her steps with a bucket and a rag. Did I stand out as suspicious here? I wiped a sweaty strand of hair out of my eyes and tried to calm my racing heart.

Nobody said a word – I'd made it! I'd done exactly what

Mom wanted and right away too! Well, I'd done half of what she wanted. Now I just had to get the case to Room 40, and we could all go back to our right time. It almost seemed too easy.

I wanted to ask Dad and Malcolm what to do with the briefcase, how to get it into Room 40, but another rule of time travel was that you couldn't bring things back with you. The only thing that traveled with me was my sketchbook. The briefcase had to stay in its own time. If I could hide it somewhere, maybe it would safely stay there until I went to the present, talked to Dad and Malcolm, then came back into the past to get it again.

But that was a huge gamble. I wasn't good enough at time travel to pinpoint exactly where and when I'd go. Whatever was in the briefcase, it was far too important to risk losing. The sky was darkening quickly, the air turning even colder, but the handle of the briefcase felt red-hot. I had to get it safely to Room 40.

I asked a boy hawking newspapers how to get to the Admiralty Building. It turned out I was in a neighborhood called Piccadilly Circus – though there were no tents or clowns or elephants, just a big traffic circle with a statue on a tall column in the center. Maybe the chaos of people and cars was the circus part. I wanted to buy one of the boy's newspapers, but without any money, all I could do was scan the front page. The main story was about British forces facing the Turks in the Sinai Peninsula in preparation for invading Palestine. My heart flipped! Was this the very beginning of Israel? From Ottoman Empire to British mandate to Jewish state? Did Mom's plan have something to do with Israel? I shook my head. It couldn't be, at least not according to Malcolm. But he didn't know that this was the big news of the day, Britain poised to advance into Palestine. I studied the newspaper for any other hints. There was an article about Russian soldiers in France, another about fighting in Roumania (I guessed they meant Romania, but that's how it was spelled). Nothing about the United States, Wilson, or German sabotage.

"Yuh wants it, yuh buys it!" the boy growled, shoving his stack of papers behind his back. "I've already give yuh summat for nuttin'." Much as I wanted to read the whole story about Palestine, all I could do was thank him and follow his directions.

If I'd understood him correctly – not at all a sure bet since his accent made that iffy – all I had to do was walk down Haymarket to Cockspur and I'd see the Admiralty Arch on my right, go through the Arch, and there I'd be. There were fewer people on the streets now as the sun set and darkness settled in. I passed by streetlights, but none of them were on. Maybe they were conserving energy. Even in sixteenth-century Rome, there were torches in sconces on buildings to help light the way at night. In nineteenth-century Paris, there were gas lamps that were lit as the sun set. Here in 1917 London, there was darkness, plain and simple.

Some light streaked from under doorways of restaurants and bars, and the moon gave a soft glow that helped guide me. I wasn't sure if the smaller street I'd turned on was Cockspur, but when I saw the enormous Arch, relief washed over me. The Admiralty

Building and the mysterious Room 40 had to be on the other side. But would anyone be there this late to let me in?

Sure enough, once I passed through the arch, I could see an impressive complex, an old-fashioned kind of Pentagon. It reminded me of the War College I'd seen in nineteenth-century Paris. The same broad-shouldered kind of building, with towers on each corner glowering down on the public. I circled around the whole enormous place, but nobody answered when I pounded on doors, rapped at

windows. Which was probably a good thing – they'd just think I was a crazy person. What kind of excuse did I have to be there after regular hours?

So, I had the briefcase. I'd found the Admiralty Building. Now what? Of course! Sylvia had given me her card, the one with her mother's address written on it, Russell Square.

I walked back through the Arch. The newsboy was gone, so I searched for an open business where I could ask for directions, but everything looked closed now, even restaurants. There were no inviting, cozy, light-filled rooms. In fact, there was still no light anywhere except for thin glimmers from under some doors. Was there some kind of power outage? It felt strange to be in such a big city with absolutely no light, as if I was in the middle of a desert or the countryside.

Above, the stars glittered bright and cold in the deepening blackness, and a strange low hum filled the air. I tried to place the odd sound – a generator? A big truck? Before I could figure anything out, three loud explosions blasted and doors flew open, revealing sudden patches of brightness as people raced outside. Seconds before, I'd been alone in the darkness, and now people swirled around me in panic. I could taste their fear, bright and metallic.

"It's the zeppelins!"

"Bomb alert!"

"They're bombing us!"

Voices shrieked and people ran past, all surging toward some stairs I hadn't noticed before, leading below the street. The Underground! People were using the subway tunnels as a bomb shelter. The humming got louder and people pushed their way through, crazed by fear. There was no such thing as women and children

Marissa Moss

first, just an animal rush for survival. I was caught up in the crowd, terrified of being trampled to death. I hugged the briefcase to my chest, trying to roll myself into a tight ball. Someone shoved me forward. Someone else shunted me to the side. A broad woman with three small children clutching tightly to her skirt offered a human shield, and I followed close behind her as she cleared a path down the stairs, yelling, "Save my chicks! My chickies, come with me!"

Secure in the subway, people stopped shoving. The woman with the children plunked herself down and gathered her crying brood onto her generous lap. I wished I could be held in the comfort of a mother's arms. Where was Mom? Was she someplace safe from the bombs? Why had she come here now, to this scary place at this dangerous time? I was furious with her and furiously afraid. A deep dread that she'd been killed seeped into me.

At least there were small lights strung along the curved tunnel walls at regular intervals, enough to allow me to see more than shadows. People were crammed in everywhere, whole families huddled together next to complete strangers. The smell of unwashed bodies, muddy clothes, and musty hair was stronger than at any school gym. It was like being inside of one of Malcolm's sweaty socks.

On one side of me slumped an old man with a bristly chin and a wool cap pulled firmly over his ears. A mushroomy-tobacco odor wafted from him. On the other, stood a boy around Malcolm's age, shivering in his knit vest, smelling of wood smoke. I guessed

he'd run out without a coat, like a lot of the people here. But there were so many bodies packed together, it was much warmer than outside. I wondered if he was shaking with fear. How safe were we down here?

"Is that why there weren't any street-lights?" I asked him, suddenly understanding the blackout conditions above ground. "So the planes won't know where to drop bombs?"

"Airplanes don't drop bombs." The boy looked at me like I was an idiot.

"Well, sorry I said anything," I snapped. "I'm an American. There's no war back at home. I didn't know what to expect in London." That was a huge understatement. Dad had said the fighting in World War I was in the trenches in France, but really it was everywhere. In the seas with German U-boats sinking passenger ships and in the air with bombs dropped on cities. I shivered myself, and not from cold.

"I didn't say you were a dolt." Which was true, he hadn't, not with words at least. "And you're right about the streetlights. We have blackout curtains at home too, so the Huns can't see where to bomb."

"But you said airplanes don't bomb." If the boy hadn't reminded me of someone, I would have given up, but there was something in his posture, something in his eyes that was familiar. He seemed like a friend, someone I could talk to. He just didn't know that yet.

"It's the zeppelins that do the bombing. The worst was in September, two years back. We lost our house in that one. Good thing you weren't here then."

Now I really did feel like an idiot. "I'm so sorry! Was anybody hurt?" This country really was at war, and not the way America went to war, where the fighting happened somewhere far away, where most of us didn't have to see it or suffer directly from it.

The boy shook his head. "We're lucky, we are." He shrugged and added, "Though it may not seem like it tonight."

I definitely didn't feel lucky. And how about Mom, was she lucky? Did she know she had asked me to come during a bombing raid? She couldn't have, she wouldn't have. But that made me wonder if I could trust her choices at all. The briefcase felt hot and heavy in my arms, a reminder of a change I'd already made.

"How often does this happen?" I asked, trying to calm the rising panic in my chest.

"Last fall was bad. But it's been quiet now for about a month. It's too foggy for the Huns to see much, plus we're careful now with lights and all."

I nodded, hoping this wasn't the beginning of a new bombing onslaught.

"Just so you know, I tried to enlist. Too young, they said." The boy sounded angry.

"Of course you're too young!" I couldn't imagine Malcolm being a soldier. "Don't worry, I'm sure the Americans will enter the war soon. We'll make a difference."

The boy stared at me intently. Looking into his gray eyes, I felt a strange sensation. Strange, but also familiar. I knew him, I recognized him from somewhere. No, from somewhen. With a jolt, I remembered this same voice, this same look to the eyes, though they were a different color then. Claude, Degas's apprentice in Paris, and then Giovanni, Caravaggio's servant in Rome. Somehow they were all related. And all of them made my stomach jittery, my breath come faster.

"What's your name?" I could feel my checks turn pink. What I really wanted to ask was who are you? Who are you really?

"Clark, Clark Warden." The boy dipped his head in a quick nod. "And you are?"

What had I told Cecily? "Miriam Lodge," I said, trying to sound casual, normal. As if I knew what that was. "I feel like we've met somewhere before. Have we?"

Clark gave me another penetrating look, then shook his head. "Don't think so. Don't know any Yanks. Unless you were British in a past life."

There was no answer to that. I let silence fill the space between us. Silence! "I don't hear any more explosions." I strained to listen. "Do you think it's okay to go back up?" Fresh air would clear up the fog of embarrassment. I couldn't help feeling like I was around an old crush, even though we'd just met.

"Those first blasts were warnings, not explosions. Before we started using the alarm rockets, people would be caught out in the open or in their homes when the bombs dropped. Much safer to be underground."

"Oh, like an air-raid siren," I said.

"No, not a siren, rockets," Clark repeated.

"Of course," I corrected myself. Air-raid sirens must be from World War II. I had to keep my history straight or I'd say something truly stupid. And then what would he think of me? "But anyway, that means no bombs fell, right? I didn't hear anything."

"Not yet." Clark sighed. All around me, people seemed worn out with worry. A haggard mother with five small children complained about rationing to her neighbor, while a young man huddled, hands over his ears, eyes round with terror. What had he lived through to make him so scared? How many bombs had already fallen, how many lives torn apart?

A horn blared from outside. People's faces sagged with relief.

"That's the all clear," Clark explained. "It's over. No bombs this time, at least not here."

I waited for the crowds to thin before following Clark's familiar form up the stairs. It was still dark, still cold, but now voices echoed through the streets as people found their way home, wishing each other a good night, a safe sleep, grateful to have escaped any harm. A solitary car drove by. A Boy Scout stood up in the back seat, blowing loud and long on a bugle.

"Really? A Boy Scout is the all-clear signal?" It seemed like a joke, but it broke the tension for me.

"Something wrong with that?" Clark asked suspiciously, as if I were anti scouting and harbored deeply unpatriotic opinions.

"No, not at all." Still, I couldn't help smiling, it seemed so silly.

"Where are you staying, if you don't mind me asking?"

"Actually, I'm not sure how to get there. Maybe you can help me?" I wasn't ready to say good-bye yet. Instead, I handed Clark the card Sylvia had given me, the one with her mother's address scribbled on it.

"Sylvia Pankhurst? You know her?" Clark seemed impressed.

"Not really. But she said I could stay with her mother, Emmeline. Do you know them, then?" I wondered if everybody had heard of them but me.

Clark shrugged. "Just what we read in the newspapers. Emmeline Pankhurst has been fighting for women to vote for almost twenty years. My mum adores her. My father detests her. Sylvia used to work with Emmeline, but they disagree about the war. Emmeline supports it, Sylvia doesn't, which is why my mum chose the mother's group over the daughter's. So does that make you a suffragette?"

"You mean, do I believe women should vote? Of course!"

Clark smiled. "And the war?"

"What about the war?"

"Do you believe we should be fighting the Germans?"

I thought about what was in the briefcase, how it might hold proof that the Germans were trying to incite Mexico to invade the United States. I thought about Malcolm, my usually peaceful brother, and how adamantly he wanted President Wilson to support England and France. I thought about zeppelins trying to bomb innocent civilians in the middle of a big city like London. And I thought about Germany taking over all of Europe. There really was only one possible answer.

I nodded. "Yes. Of course."

"Then I would be delighted to walk you to Mrs. Pankhurst's." Clark offered his arm gallantly.

I took his arm, careful not to snuggle up against him, though I was tempted. His voice in the darkness was Claude's. His posture was Giovanni's. Being with him was like being with an old friend. Well, a little more than a friend. Good thing there was no light, so he couldn't tell I was blushing again as I remembered my almost-kiss with Claude.

"So what are you doing in London?" Clark asked. "Doesn't seem like a good time for a visit."

"There was some unpleasantness at home, so I've come to live with my aunt here." I decided to stick to the story I'd given Sylvia. Lying was complicated enough without having to keep track of which lie had been told to whom. It was easier to tell everyone the same big wad of lies.

"Is Mrs. Pankhurst your aunt then?"

"No, it's just chance that I'm staying with her." I explained how I'd stumbled upon the protest, how I'd met Sylvia, how she'd kindly offered her mother's home.

"That's a bit of luck you've had, then," Clark noted. "Would you be sleeping in the Underground elsewise?"

I was tired of staying ahead of his curiosity, figuring out what I could safely say. So I started asking things myself, a useful diversion tactic I'd learned at school when teachers asked hard questions. Besides, I genuinely wanted to know. Clark told me about his parents and the grocery store they ran, about his three brothers fighting in the trenches, his older sister driving an ambulance. It turned out to be a long walk, at least an hour through streets that got quieter and emptier the further we went. I pressed Clark to tell me more about the war, but he didn't want to talk about his brothers' experiences any more than I wanted to describe my invented family.

Instead, he gave me a kind of headline news version of major events. The terrible Battle of the Somme, stretching on for nearly five months, leaving hundreds of thousands  of British and French soldiers dead. The first use of chemical weapons at Ypres two years ago by the Germans, more proof of their cruelty if I needed any, and the shell-shocked soldiers he'd seen at the train station as the wounded returned from the Battle of Verdun last month. And we talked about America, about how the Germans sank the *Lusitania*, how they attacked cargo ships.

"How can your president allow those kinds of attacks and not fight back?" he asked. "I just don't understand that!"

It didn't make sense to me either. If those things happened today, there'd be no waiting, no patiently turning the other cheek. What kind of man was President Wilson anyway, that he could ignore that kind of assault?

As we talked, the briefcase felt heavier and heavier, as if I were carrying the weight of history, the burden of what I needed to do. Could I really change the course of the war? Should I?

"It's pretty late," Clark said as we entered a tidy little

square, like the place where Mary Poppins worked. A green, neatly trimmed park with a wrought-iron fence was ringed by houses on all sides, white and square and even, like a child's wooden toy village.

"It's not like I was expected for dinner or anything. I just hope they'll let me stay here."

"You can stay with us, you know. Our place is small, but there's a divan you could curl up on."

"That's very kind of you, but I can't." I was truly touched. I wished I could forget about Mom and just be with Clark.

"I'll at least wait and see if you can really stay here, shall I?"

"Yes, please do. And if I do stay here, can you please give me your address so I can see you again? I don't know anybody else in London." Maybe, just maybe I'd have a chance to see him again.

Clark smiled. "Of course. Do you have a pen and paper in that bag you're carrying?"

I didn't dare open the case in front of anybody, even Clark, so I reached into my pocket instead. Yes, they were still there, my notebook and pen. I'd been sketching in the subway tunnel and worried I might have dropped them.

I set the briefcase down, holding it tightly between my legs. Not very ladylike, but I wasn't letting go of something so important. I found a blank page and waited for Clark to dictate.

"Forty-two Coventry Road, ask for the Wardens."

"I'll look for you later, then," I said, capping my fountain pen and tucking it and the notebook back into my pocket. I knew as I said it that it was probably a lie, no matter how much I wished it could be true. Most likely, I'd be back with Malcolm and Dad instead. And really, it would be better that way, though it didn't feel like that now.

"Tomorrow?" Clark raised a hopeful eyebrow and stood off to the side while I climbed up the short staircase to the glossy black door and rapped the knocker.

"Soon, let's say." Tomorrow was a tricky word for me.

A maid opened the door, dressed in a white apron with a stiff white cap, like an upside down paper muffin cup on her head.

"Yes, miss?"

"I'm here to see Mrs. Pankhurst. Her daughter Sylvia sent me."

"Please come in." The maid opened the door wide and gestured into the lit hallway.

I turned back to wave at Clark, sad to leave him. "I'll be fine," I called. "Good night and thank you!" Would I ever see him again? Maybe in a completely different time and place?

The door shut behind me and the maid led me into a room she called the parlor.

"Please wait here while I tell Mrs. Pankhurst you've come, miss. Miss?"

"Miss Miriam Lodge," I said, handing her the card Sylvia had given me, as if proof of my right to be there. "From the United States." Sylvia said her mother had visited America, so maybe that would make me a more valuable guest.

"Of course, miss."

I was alone in a room that looked like something from one of my mom's BBC TV shows: porcelain knickknacks on the fireplace mantle, paintings of dogs and horses and landscapes on the walls, overstuffed chairs with high backs and tables with spindly legs that looked highly breakable. But there were also Japanese prints and fans, as well as Chinese ceramics, marking the home of a world traveler. It was the kind of room where you would perch on a chair, rather than sink into one. I sat stiffly, afraid I'd shatter something valuable, the briefcase set solidly between by feet. I glanced at the still-closed doors, nervous about meeting Mrs. Pankhurst, but even more edgy thinking about the briefcase. This was my first chance to look inside, to see if it really had the incriminating documents Morton thought were there. What if he'd pointed out the wrong man? What if the tall man wasn't a spy after all? What if he wasn't even German?

Before I could peek, the door opened and a gray-haired woman with a strong jaw and no-nonsense gaze swept into the room. I bounced up from my seat – it seemed rude to stay seated in front of her.

"Good evening, Miss Lodge, and welcome." Mrs. Pankhurst gestured for me to sit and arranged herself on a yellow print chair. I've heard women described as handsome before, but that had never made sense to me. All it had meant was not beautiful, not pretty, not cute, not lovely. When I saw Mrs. Pankhurst, I finally understood it. She was handsome in a proud, forceful way, with a strong jaw and broad forehead, deep-set, intelligent eyes, her skin still pale and smooth though she was older than Mom, old enough to have grown daughters. She didn't look anything like Sylvia, whose features seemed vague and half-finished compared to her imposing mother.

"Millicent will bring us some tea. Should she set out a cold supper for you? Have you eaten yet?"

Suddenly I was starving. "You're very kind to offer. I hate to impose, but your daughter Sylvia said I should come. I don't have anywhere else to go." I stared at the oriental carpet under my feet.

What if she said no? Really, why let a complete stranger into your house? Would Mom ever do that? Would Dad? I should have stayed with Clark when he'd offered.

"It's no imposition at all. Sylvia knows that our home is always open to women in need. It would be hypocritical to advocate for woman's suffrage while ignoring the plight of individual women."

My shoulders slumped in relief. "You're very kind!" An awkward silence followed. Clearly I was supposed to say something more. "I admire your work for women to vote," I offered. "It's not fair that they can't."

"It's a beastly injustice, yes, for all of us." Mrs. Pankhurst leaned forward. "Perhaps you know Alice Paul? She's demonstrated with us, been arrested with us."

I felt like I was failing an important test. The name was vaguely familiar – had Sylvia mentioned her? I wished I knew more about the history of women getting the vote, both in the United States and in England, but I had to admit, it was a right I totally took for granted. Of course women could vote, of course they should be able to. How could people have ever considered them less human than men, less capable?

"I take it you don't have much at stake in the issue?" Mrs. Pankhurst pressed on.

"Why do you say that?" Just because I didn't know who Alice Paul was?

"You refer to women as 'they,' as if you don't include yourself. You can't vote, either, can you?"

So that was my mistake! It was funny, I hadn't included myself because once I turned eighteen, of course I'd vote. But in 1917, I wouldn't have that chance. Not in England, not in America.

"I've given you the wrong impression!" I tried to repair the damage. "I strongly believe that women should vote. It's absolutely wrong that we can't. But as you know, the situation is different in America. There are no violent political protests like you have here." At least according to Sylvia that was true. Once again, I needed to know history better! When we'd covered this period in American history, there'd been a sentence or two about women and voting rights, barely anything.

Before I could make any more mistakes, the maid came back with a tray. Tea, naturally, but also crustless sandwiches cut into triangles. The sight of the food made me even hungrier, but I tried to take small bites the way a young lady should. I'd hoped for peanut better, but the goop between the bread had a distinctly fishy taste. I was hungry, but not *that* hungry.

"I won't badger you with questions," Mrs. Pankhurst said, sipping tea from a gilt-edged cup. "I respect your privacy completely, so there's no need to tell me anything about what brings you to England or your problems at home. Unless, and here I must be clear,

I'm afraid, unless there's any fear of danger, of violence. I've had angry husbands pound on my door, looking for their fleeing wives. If that's your situation, I do need to know."

I almost choked on my tea. "I'm only fourteen!" I gasped.

"I've sheltered wives who were barely twelve. We haven't changed that law yet, though we will."

Ick! My skin crawled at the thought of being married to some hairy, nasty old man. I pictured somebody with thick hairs sprouting from his nostrils, a wobbly chin, and a saggy beer belly. I must have looked as disgusted as I felt, because Mrs. Pankhurst gently pressed my arm.

"There's no shame in such a disagreeable marriage. You had no choice. And you were brave enough to get away. That's more than many a girl can say."

"I'm not married! And nobody will come looking for me here, I'm sure of it." But even as I said it, I thought of the Watcher who was chasing after Mom, trying to stop her from breaking the Rules of time travel. Was she looking for me too? She was certainly scary, but as a beautiful young woman, she wasn't someone Mrs. Pankhurst would consider a threat.

I couldn't tell if Mrs. Pankhurst believed me, but she changed the subject, talking instead about her struggles to convince Parliament to give women the vote. She'd been arrested more than a dozen times, gone on hunger strikes and been force-fed, from her description a torture worse than waterboarding. "This is what Americans don't understand," she insisted. "We've presented petitions to the government and in exchange been treated like criminals. We've asked politely and been answered with brutality. What other recourse do we have?

"Now, though, with the war, it's more important to focus on supporting our soldiers. Once we've defeated the savage Germans, we can work once more on justice for everyone, voting rights for all."

I nodded my head, sipped tea, and nodded some more. I could tell that Mrs. Pankhurst expected outrage, but I was too exhausted to muster much. I tried to blink myself awake, to pay attention, but I found myself slumping into the stiff chair, my stomach warmed with tea.

"My dear, I've talked you into a stupor! Forgive my manners, I do get carried away on the subject. Millicent will show you to your room and we'll talk more in the morning."

"Thank you for all your kindness," I murmured, remembering to clutch the briefcase as I followed the maid up a flight of stairs, down a hall, into a small, tidy room. I meant to look in the briefcase, to see what secrets it held, but as soon as I lay down on the bed, my eyes closed and that's all I remembered.

January 17, 1917

Thin rays of morning light woke me up. I stumbled out of the unfamiliar bed, searching for the briefcase. Yes, it was still there, right where I'd left it, and now, at last, I opened it, heart pounding. But when I took out the piles of papers, I couldn't understand any of them. They were in German – of course! What did I expect from a German spy? I sorted through the pages, hoping to make sense of something, but I'd studied French in school.

"Breakfast, miss," the maid called through the closed door.

"I'll be right down," I said, shoving the papers back into the briefcase and sliding it under the bed.

I ran over the story I'd told Sylvia, the one I'd told Clark, so that for once I'd be prepared with a quick and ready lie.

"Good morning," Mrs. Pankhurst greeted me when I walked into the dining room. She was seated at the table, already midway through a soft-boiled egg. More soft-boiled eggs, sausages, and small fried fish were set out on a side board, while the table held a rack with toast slices (like dishes in a dish drainer!), saucers of jam and butter, and a tea pot.

"Good morning! Thank you so much for having me. The room is very comfortable." I looked at  the array of food, my stomach grumbling. I couldn't face the fish (again!) or sausage so early in the morning, or maybe ever. But eggs and toast seemed normal enough, along with a cup of tea. That was the easy part. The table was set with a confusing array of forks, spoons, and knives, like some kind of social test. Would I know which fork to use? Was there a different one for eggs than for fish? A special sausage fork?

"Perhaps now that you've had a good night's rest, you can tell me your plans."

I'd practiced for this only a short while ago, but the silverware distracted me. What had I told Clark? Stories about poison gas and trench warfare jumbled around in my head, but that was what he'd told me, not what I'd told him.

"I'd like to find a job," I finally said, deciding that the easiest thing to do would be to skip the eggs entirely. The toast was easy — I'd use my hands. "Someone on the train mentioned a position as a maid or a cleaning person in the Admiralty Building. Could you give me directions so I could try there?" As soon as the words were out of my mouth, I remembered that I'd told her daughter that my cousin worked there and that was why I needed to go to the Admiralty Building. Good thing she and Sylvia weren't getting along. They weren't likely to see each other soon. I watched my hostess, hoping for a clue to toast etiquette. If only I weren't hungry! Then I'd just get directions to the Admiralty Building and flee the trap of the table entirely!

Mrs. Pankhurst raised an eyebrow. "Odd place for a position. And you mean to be in service?" She sliced precisely into a silvery fish. Ugh! Now I knew which were the right utensils for that task, which was no help to me at all.

"I need to earn a living, don't I?" Could I add the bit about my cousin now? I could say I'd heard from him they were hiring. Lying was such a messy business. But it was easier than navigating through British table manners! Mrs. Pankhurst laid her knife down across the top of her plate and, as if that were a secret signal, the maid swooped in and cleared away the dish, quickly replacing it with a clean one.

"An educated young lady working as a maid? That may happen in your country, but it simply isn't done here. You could be a governess, perhaps a secretary. There are factory jobs with all the men away at war, but that work is for the lower classes, not for you."

I bet I didn't seem high class, either. Maybe Americans were a class of their own. I gingerly picked up a different knife than the fish one, hoping I'd chosen correctly. "I thought you were a social-ist, that you helped poor working women." I slathered some butter on my toast and quickly set the knife down. Mission accomplished!

"I do, which is how I know you aren't one of them. You may have fallen on hard times, but you aren't that class and you won't be welcome among them. The other women will view you with suspicion, consider you a toff who's taking food out of their mouths." Mrs. Pankhurst took her own slice of toast and spread butter and jam on it – with another knife completely.

So despite my knife blunder – or because of it? – I was a toff, whatever that was. "Then perhaps a job as a secretary, like you say. I can type." As soon as I said it, I wondered if the typewriter had been invented yet. Mrs. Pankhurst would think I was rude and stupid! I needed a cheat-sheet list of inventions and dates.

telephone typewriter airplane electric light

umbrella car toaster

Plus a list of my lies for easy reference.

"If that's what you would like, I may be able to help you. There's a reception this afternoon being held by several publishers for their writers. Since I published my memoir three years ago, I'm invited, and you can come as my guest. I'll introduce you to some editors. One of them may need your services. With so many men gone, it's likely."

"That's generous of you," I said, trying to contain my excitement at the idea of being part of a literary circle, even for just a couple of hours. I took a congratulatory bite of toast. "Does that mean I'll meet some other writers?"

Mrs. Pankhurst smiled and started cutting up her own toast with a knife and fork, as if she were eating a steak, not a grilled piece of bread. I dropped my toast back on the plate.

"My publisher, Eveleigh Nash, works with a fine list of writers, many of whom will be present. And William Heinemann will be there with his distinguished authors."

Heinemann? That's where Malcolm had said Nigel de Grey worked. Maybe he'd be at the reception and I could simply hand him the briefcase! This might be the easiest, quickest mission yet, the one that finally got Mom home where she belonged. And I wouldn't even need to go to the mysterious Room 40.

As I awkwardly cut up my toast (didn't British people eat

anything with their hands beside tiny sandwiches?), I realized I hadn't said anything about my hostess being a writer. That wasn't the kind of thing a polite guest would ignore. "You wrote a memoir?" I asked, trying to make up for my mistake. "About your protests, that kind of thing?"

"Essentially, yes. It's about our struggles getting the government to listen to us, about the cruel treatment of women in our society and the changes which must be made."

"But it's not over," I said. "You wrote the book before you won the vote." I'd done it again, been the tactless American. Why did I blurt out these kinds of things?

"The book was meant to help our cause, to educate the public as to why we've been willing to burn buildings, destroy property, disrupt events. And it has done that, though not as much as I would have hoped."

"I'd love to read a copy, if I may." I hoped that adding the "if I may" made me sound more polite. I nibbled on a forkful of toast. Eaten this way, like a main dish, it was strangely more filling.

"I didn't know you were so interested in women's suffrage." Mrs. Pankhurst studied her plate as she said this, carefully not looking at me. I was probably too rude for her to bear.

"All women should be able to vote, work in whatever job they want, and have the same rights as men. One day there will be women in government, in positions of power." I thought of the British prime minister, Margaret Thatcher, and the movie version of her life, the one with Meryl Streep. I smiled, thinking how much I could tell Mrs. Pankhurst if that kind of thing was allowed. Which, obviously, was another Rule – No Talking about Future Events.

"I'm delighted to hear such passion from you! It's young people like you who can make the difference, you know."

"Yes, exactly! Yes, we can!" If my hostess wanted enthusiasm, I could give her plenty. I thought of that famous poster from World War II, the one of a woman with a kerchief around her head, her muscle flexed, with the slogan "We Can Do It!"

"You know, I met your daughter Sylvia at a rally for women getting the vote. She was speaking, along with Mary Richardson. They both said wonderful things about you!" Now I felt I'd proved myself. After all, Mrs. Pankhurst didn't know how I'd met Sylvia – it could have been at a tea party, something not at all political.

"So you don't know Sylvia well?" She sipped her tea.

"I just met her that one time," I admitted.

"Long enough, I wager, that she told you we've parted ways. It's practically the first thing she tells anyone she meets these days." Mrs. Pankhurst sighed heavily.

"She mentioned something about your support for the war, which she disagrees with, that's all." Maybe this was my chance to get the full story. I dabbed at my mouth with the linen napkin, watching Mrs. Pankhurst for clues about table manners. No elbows on the table, no gulping, no talking with your mouth full, no having a mouth full in the first place. There was something about Mrs. Pankhurst that made me worry about all that. She may have been the leader of a violent protest group, but she carried herself like a lady, all stiff upper lip and that sort of thing. Sylvia was more ordinary, more like a shopkeeper or a teacher, a regular kind of person.

"My daughter always has to do things her own way. It's a pity, because we could accomplish so much more united than we can divided. Fortunately, I still have my oldest daughter, Christabel, at my side. Right now she's in France, working with our partners on the continent. It's a shame you can't meet her."

"I hope to have the chance someday," I murmured, not any wiser about why they'd fought, but feeling like I was in the middle of a family feud. I felt a rush of affection for Malcolm. He would never compete with me for Dad or for Mom. We were a team. Our family worked together, like now, trying to figure out what Mom needed and how to do it. Even if we couldn't talk to Mom, we knew she was away for our sakes, not on some mission of her own.

The publishing reception wasn't until four, and there was no guarantee that Nigel de Grey would be there, so after breakfast, I washed up quickly, put my less-than-fresh clothes back on, and headed out with the briefcase to retrace my steps to the Admiralty Building. In the morning light, the streets looked almost cheerful, washed clean of the terror of the bombing raid. As I left behind the careful row houses with their neat gates and scrubbed sidewalks, I came to a busier part of the city. Shops, offices, restaurants lined the way, the sidewalks crowded with barrels of goods. I could almost forget there was a war on until I came to a sudden gap filled with rubble.

"What happened here?" I asked the shopkeeper next to the avalanche of brick, glass shards, tile, and dirt. The man was lining up crates of nails by the door of his hardware store.

"Bomb," he answered tersely.

"Last night!" I gasped.

"Last December," he said.

"Was anybody hurt?"

"Two people killed."

"I'm so sorry," I murmured to the man. He set down the crate without a word and went back into the store, as if bombs were part of the normal routine. Maybe they were. I clenched the briefcase tighter, more determined than ever to get it to Room 40. I strode quickly the rest of the way, through the now-familiar Arch, and found myself once again in front of the Admiralty Building. In the light of day, soldiers flanked either side of the main entrance. Would they buy the cousin-working-there story? Would looking for a job be more believable?

I squared my shoulders, preparing to be totally convincing. A teenager could be looking for a job, why not? I took a deep breath and walked up to the door, hoping the soldiers would let me pass by, unquestioned.

No such luck.

"What business do you have here?" the soldier on the right asked.

"I was told to come here for a position." Which wasn't a total lie. Mrs. Pankhurst had suggested something like that.

"Do you have an appointment?" asked the soldier on the left.

"Not exactly. But I was told to come by Mrs. Pankhurst." If she was so famous, a little name-dropping couldn't hurt.

"Mrs. Pankhurst? What office is she in?" Mr. Left glared at me.

"I don't know exactly, but she works for the war effort." This wasn't going at all well.

"We all work for the war effort," snapped Mr. Right.

"No entry without an appointment," Mr. Left declared.

"This is very important! I have to see. . . I have to see. . ." I sputtered the name of the only person I knew of inside, "Nigel de Grey!"

"Nigel de Grey?" The soldiers exchanged a look. Not a welcoming look, either. A highly suspicious look, in fact.

"Your name?" asked Mr. Left.

"Miriam Lodge," I muttered, knowing I'd blown it. I should have said I was Sylvia Pankhurst — that would have at least got me through the door before someone realized I wasn't her. I should have thought this all through more carefully.

"I'll see if he's available to see you," said Mr. Right.

"Please don't bother, I should have called first, we hadn't set an exact time, I'll telephone him for an appointment," I babbled, backing away. What were my options now? I walked around the building, hoping for a rear entrance, but I didn't see any that were open. If I didn't find Mr. de Grey at the publishers' reception, I'd have to ask Mrs. Pankhurst for a reference, a way into the building. She had to know somebody!

I stomped away, furious at myself. Malcolm had made it sound so easy — just get a job as a cleaning person. As if I could simply waltz into a military office in war time!

But I had the briefcase. That had to be my ticket in. Of course! I could say Mr. de Grey had lost his briefcase, left it on a bus maybe, and I was returning it. Why didn't I say that? I couldn't go back and say that now, it would sound stupid. Maybe I could wait until the guards changed shifts and try again? But I hadn't seen any guards there at night. Who knew how long those same men would be there.

The safest bet would be to try tomorrow. The whole scenario played in my head as I walked back past the bombed-out building. I'd tell the sentries that I'd met Mr. de Grey at my home the evening before (that is, tonight), we'd spoken about the position, and he'd left his briefcase behind by mistake, so here I was the next day (that is, tomorrow), bringing it back to him. It might actually work, and in the meanwhile, there was the chance I'd see him at the reception.

I was so focused on my thoughts, I almost didn't notice her, but something, some inner alarm bell, made me stop and scan the street ahead. The hair prickled on the back of my neck as if a ghost were nearby. Only it wasn't a ghost – it was the Watcher. Her back was to me, but I knew it was her. I just knew. I darted into a store selling stationery and stared out the window. Yes, the woman in the soft lilac cloak was turning slowly now. Did she sense me the same way I sensed her? There was her chiseled profile, the familiar sharp beauty. She wasn't alone this time. A tall, thin man swiveled beside her. I gasped.

It was the German spy, the man I'd taken the briefcase from. The Watcher was working with him? But then she was breaking her own rules, interfering with history herself. Or she was using the man to take care of her problems. Me. And Mom. I thought of how she'd set up political agitators to kill Emile Zola in Paris. How she'd used the Inquisition to finish off Giordano Bruno in Rome. I had to warn Mom!

I held my breath, stepping back into the store's shadows as the Watcher and the spy scanned the street, their eyes like laser beams right on the spot where I'd stood seconds before.

"May I help you, miss?" a nasal voice boomed in my ear like a blaring alarm. I almost dropped the briefcase.

"You startled me!" I squawked, finding myself suddenly next to a ferret-faced young man with a glistening forehead and an earnest "let-me-please-please-you" look.

"I'm dreadfully sorry, miss, but as you came into this establishment, I thought you might be looking for something. Perhaps some stationery?"

"Um." I swallowed nervously. I couldn't leave yet, that was for sure. "Yes, actually. I mean, no, not stationery, but perhaps a notebook." I didn't have any money. There was no question of buying anything except time.

"A notebook?" The clerk's Adam's apple bobbed up and down. Was he as nervous as me? I eyed him carefully. Could he be a Watcher too? How would I know? What if I were surrounded by Watchers?

I pushed down the panic bubbling into my throat, telling myself I was being totally ridiculous. Maybe it was the clerk's first day. Maybe he was just an anxious personality. Or maybe I had to get out of there!

I glanced out the window. The Watcher was still there, along with the spy. They'd come closer, in fact, and looked like they were about to go into a nearby store, one with hats in the window. Were they searching each shop?

"Do you mean a journal or a diary?"

"I mean a notebook!" I snapped, swiveling to look back at the clerk, then out the window again. In that split second between glances, the Watcher had disappeared. She and the spy had to be in the hat shop. I had to get out of here quick, before they searched this store.

"Forget it, I'll look somewhere else," I said to the miserable clerk and started to push open the door. Oh, no! There they were, out on the street again.

"Or maybe not," I gasped, backing into the store.

"If the young lady would be patient, I'm sure I could find something pleasing. We have some exceptional stock in the back. If you could wait one small moment." The clerk darted behind a curtain closing off the storeroom. Was there a back exit through there?

"I'll look with you!" I pushed aside the curtain, ignoring the young man's shocked gaping. Clearly no customer was supposed to set foot back there, but I was breaking far more important rules. I scanned the crowded room quickly-- a desk, a file cabinet, shelves piled high with paper goods, a tray with a tea set, and yes, a door, a way out, I hoped, not a staff bathroom.

"Is that the time?" I shrilled. "I'm so sorry! I must be going or my mistress will have my skin." If he was really a Watcher, I'd find out now. I didn't wait for permission, but shoved past the astonished clerk and thrust the door open. Yes! There was my exit, a narrow alleyway, lined with nasty-smelling rubbish. The clerk stood frozen, dazed by my horrible rudeness. So he wasn't a Watcher after all, just a guy eager to make a sale who was appalled by my lack of manners.

I ran out, welcoming the gloom, the rancid smells, even the darting motion of a rat, and kept running through the warren of streets until the stitch in my side made me stop for a quick rest. I didn't care how crazy I looked. I just wanted to get as far from the Watcher as possible.

By the time I got back to Mrs. Pankhurst's house, the briefcase was a lead weight in my arms, my dress was plastered to me with sticky sweat, and the sun was a hazy smudge high overhead in the cloudy sky. It had to be noon, but that left several hours before the reception. Enough time for me to calm down, to think things through clearly. What did the Watcher know? Where would she be now? And was she the only one? Was the spy also a Watcher? Did I have to start worrying that there were Watchers all around me? I stared at the houses in the tidy little square. They all looked so proper. Could someone be spying at me from one of their lace-trimmed windows? I shuddered. What about Mom? Was she safe?

It all felt like too much. Too much responsibility, too much fear, too much worry. My cheeks were wet with tears, even though I wasn't sad. I was terrified and furious, both at once. I wanted it to stop, all of it. Couldn't Mom just come home and stop sending me on these horrible missions, forcing me to take these terrible risks?

Except she wasn't making me do anything. She was asking. And I chose to say yes. But did I really have a choice? If I said no, it meant losing Mom, maybe forever.

I took a deep breath. I'd see this through, that's all there was to it.

The maid let me in, saying that Mrs. Pankhurst would be away until three, but luncheon had been set out for me in the dining room. I was sweaty and filthy, an emotional mess, and more than any of those – hungry. Food. Plus no worries about silverware, so I could simply eat. I just prayed there'd be no fish involved.

There was. But there was also a tureen of soup that didn't smell disgusting, a plate of cheese, slices of bread, and something that looked turnip-like. I skipped the turnip and fish, but filled myself with everything else. It wasn't delicious, but it wasn't nasty, either. Remembering how the woman in the subway had complained about rationing and food shortages, I really couldn't complain.

As I ate, I calmed down. Under all the anger and fear, I actually felt lucky, lucky to have seen the Watcher before she saw me. Was I fine-tuning my time travel abilities? I had definitely felt her before I saw her, like an electric current hitting me with a warning shock.

Maybe, just maybe, I was getting better at all this.

But how could I warn Mom? Or did she already know? She

must. Really, my only way to help her was to take the briefcase where she wanted, so she'd come back to our right time. For once and for all!

After finishing lunch, I hid the briefcase back under the bed and washed my face, hands, and armpits quickly, hoping I didn't stink. My nerves were still so jangly, I had to do something besides wait for the reception, so I decided to look for a copy of Mrs. Pankhurst's book. There had to be a reason I was in this house, and her book might tell me what it was. It could be just the connection to the publishers' reception, to Nigel de Grey, but I had a hunch there was something more. Something to do with her relationship with Sylvia, with the mother-daughter split. And I was trusting my hunches now, more than ever.

The book might be in the parlor, though I didn't remember seeing any bookshelves there. I padded quietly downstairs and almost bumped into a maid, carrying a neatly folded pile of linens.

"Do you need something, miss?" she asked, gathering her tipping pile into a firmly held stack.

"I just thought I'd read Mrs. Pankhurst's book, the one she wrote about her struggles for the vote."

"I'm sure there's a copy in the library, miss, the door ahead on your left."

Here was something I loved about this time and place — having a personal library! Mrs. Pankhurst's home was solidly comfortable, but she wasn't rich. Still, there it was, through the door indicated by the maid – a room just for books, lined with shelves floor to ceiling. A ladder on wheels leaned against one wall, so that you could reach even the highest shelves. A couple of overstuffed reading chairs – comfortable, not spindly, like in the formal parlor – a desk, and a small sofa were the only furniture. Most of the room was filled with one thing – books. It even smelled like books, that wonderful aroma of fresh-baked cloth, ink, and paper, all mixed together.

Curious about what kinds of things Mrs. Pankhurst read, I scanned the book titles. I loved to do this when Mom and Dad dragged us to people's homes for dinner. You could tell a lot about someone by what they read. Plus looking at books was more interesting than answering the predictable questions about how I liked school, what was my favorite class, did I play any sports. Our house was full of photography art books, thick books on history, badly designed paperbacks on computer coding and programs (like even the books about such a boring subject had to look dull), and lots and lots of novels. Mrs. Pankhurst had shelves full of Greek and Roman classics, histories, political treatises, French novels, dictionaries. Dictionaries!

Yes, there it was, right next to the French dictionary, a German-English dictionary. This was my chance to see what the papers in the briefcase said. I wouldn't be able to read them fluently, but I could at least tell how – or if – they were important for Room 40.

I slipped the dictionary off the shelf. Nobody was in the hallway when I peeked out the door, so I ran out and up the stairs, back to my room. Not that a maid would care if I borrowed a book, but it seemed better to avoid awkward questions and unnecessary lies.

I pulled out the briefcase from its hiding place and took out the papers, trying to guess which were the most important. Some featured lists of numbers, but otherwise there was nothing marking any one paper as more distinctive. I took one at random and started

flipping through the dictionary.

What a mouthful German was! Many words were five or six syllables long. And the verbs came only at the end of a sentence, so I'd translate a long stream of nouns, prepositions, adjectives without understanding the action of it all until the very end. It was painstaking, but when I first figured out that several pages detailed payments to someone named Lothar Witzke, a man living in the United States, I knew I'd found something important. Then I saw "New Jersey" and "Black Tom" and "explosion," and a shiver ran through me. The Germans had plotted some kind of explosion at a munitions depot in New York Harbor. Had Clark mentioned something like that?

I couldn't tell if it had already happened or was only in the planning stages. Then I saw "California" and blood rushed into my head. The Germans were planning some kind of attack in my home state! I read through the papers in a rush, my eyes blurry with panic. Where in California? What? Was this what Mom needed to stop from happening?

There were details about devices, detonators, targets, but I skipped past them, searching for a place name. Then I caught one – Mare Island Shipyard. Mare Island? It sounded vaguely familiar. Was it close to Berkeley, where we lived? Or maybe it was in Southern California, near Los Angeles.

A rapping on the door startled me. "Miss," the maid called. "Madam is leaving shortly for the reception. She has a dress here for you."

"I'll be right there!" I shoved the papers quickly back into the briefcase, washed my face again at the washstand. A dress? That was a relief, considering how wrinkled and dusty my clothes looked. I opened the door and before I could say anything, the maid marched in and started unbuttoning my dress.

"I can do this myself!" I protested.

The maid looked astonished, but she stood and watched silently as my thick, clumsy fingers fumbled with the row of fine buttons. I could feel anxious sweat pooling under my arms and at the back of my neck as the buttons refused to budge.

"If you please, miss," the maid insisted. Her fingers flew along the stubborn buttons and she quickly had the grimy dress off and the new, clean one on, laced and buttoned.

"This was Miss Sylvia's when she was younger," explained the maid. "It suits your complexion."

I turned to gape in the mirror. I actually looked pretty wearing the crushed blue velvet dress with a lacy white collar.

"And now, miss, your hair." This time I didn't stop her as the maid set me in the chair and started brushing my hair. Memories of when I was a very little girl, so little Mom brushed my hair for me, filled me with a lulling calm.

"You look lovely, miss," the maid said when she'd set in the last hairpin.

I did. I smiled at my reflection. Too bad Clark couldn't see me now.

"I'll leave you then, miss, but come downstairs when you're ready. Mrs. Pankhurst will be waiting for you."

I looked around the room, wondering if I should take the briefcase. It seemed odd to carry something like that now that I was nicely dressed. But what if Nigel de Grey would be there?

With shaking fingers, I took out the pages that seemed the most incriminating, the ones mentioning Mare Island, and folded them into my pocket. It would be easier, more natural, to offer some pages to an editor, wouldn't it? I could even say they were an essay or a short story I wanted his opinion on.

"Thank you for the dress!" I gushed to Mrs. Pankhurst as I came downstairs. "And I love your book!" I hadn't read a word of it, but I could guess she'd have described prison, the kind of things she'd already told me. "I didn't realize how ugly everything was. I mean, still is. How brave you and the other suffragists had to be."

"It isn't a question of courage so much as of determination. We did, and we continue to do, what's necessary."

I thought of that. Was that what I was doing? I certainly wasn't brave, but I was trying very hard to do the right thing. The trouble was, I wasn't always sure what that was. But I was beginning to feel that maybe that was the hardest part of doing the right thing – figuring out what that was to begin with.

A carriage waited outside for us, pulled by horses. Alongside it stood a familiar figure – Clark!

I could feel my cheeks heat up. I'd just been thinking about him, wanting him to see how pretty I could be, and now here he was.

"Miss Miriam." He smiled while I tried to calm my flustered face. "I came by to see if you'd like to come out with me for tea."

A date? He was asking me on a date! I wanted to say yes. I almost did. But instead I sputtered, "That's kind of you, but as you see, I'm going out now with Mrs. Pankhurst."

"Tomorrow then?" He looked so friendly and hopeful, I hated to disappoint him – and myself. In another life, at another time, I'd have jumped at the chance. But I'd already hurt Claude and upset Giovanni. I told myself I wasn't going to get involved with anyone else that way. It would be selfish.

Mrs. Pankhurst interrupted my thoughts. "We must be going now, Miriam. You'll have to excuse us, young man."

"I'm so sorry, Clark," I mumbled. "I don't know about tomorrow. I may not be here by then."

"Of course, I didn't mean to impose." His face darkened. I felt like I'd slapped him.

I slumped into the carriage, my stomach twisting sourly. Clark walked away, shoulders stiff with hurt. He didn't look back once.

"What do you think of automobiles?" I asked Mrs. Pankhurst, lamely changing the subject.

"An astonishing invention." She smiled, graciously pretending Clark had never been there. "In some ways, we're moving forward very quickly, while in others, we're standing still."

I sank into the leather seats, trying to enjoy the view, the streets full of people, the swirl of life around me. I let  the clip-clop sound of the horse's hooves wash over me, rock me like a lullaby. I had to forget about Clark and focus on finding Nigel de Grey. I felt for the papers in my pocket, reassured that they were still there. Touching them, I remembered Mare Island, the planned explosion. That was way more important than any boy.

The reception was being held in a fancy hotel, the kind with uniformed men wearing lots of gold braid guarding the entrance. Unlike the soldiers at the Admiralty Building, these men didn't question anybody. They unfolded the steps from the carriages, helped out the ladies, held canes and top hats for the men. Then they opened the doors wide and ushered us in.

This was wealth, real riches. The floor of the atrium was polished marble, the ceilings high and covered with paintings of mythological scenes in pale pinks and blues, like a giant candy box lid over our heads. I didn't think publishers would be in such a ritzy place. I'd been imagining a signing at a bookstore, that kind of thing.

I was grateful for the borrowed dress all over again. I adjusted my collar, proud of how I looked next to Mrs. Pankhurst, dressed in an elegant burgundy dress, with long white gloves, a thin diamond choker, and black hat with a plume the same color as her dress. She took my arm, leading me into a ballroom off one side of the main hall.

The ballroom was even

more magnificent, lined with gilt mirrors and tapestries set in the paneled walls. Immense chandeliers glittered overhead. People as fancy as the surroundings filled the room. The men wore formal suits, shiny black and white, so stiff and proper, it looked like the clothes were wearing the men instead of the other way around. In contrast to the crisp black and white of the men, the women looked like a flock of exotic birds in their rich array of brightly colored gloves, gowns, and jewelry. Serious jewels, the kind you'd see in a museum – sapphires, emeralds, diamonds, rubies, and pearls, swirling in gold and silver around their necks, arms, and fingers, dripping from their ears, and some even set in tiaras in their hair. You wouldn't know there was a war going on from the way they swanned around, looking like royalty.

I trotted nervously at Mrs. Pankhurst's side, searching faces for someone who looked like a Nigel, but to be honest, all the men looked like Nigels. The room was already abuzz with conversation so we must have been fashionably late. It was the only thing fashionable about me.

"I'll introduce you to the first writer we come across, but then I'm afraid you'll be on your own for a bit," Mrs. Pankhurst murmured. "I'll make sure you meet an editor or two before we leave so you can ask about a position."

"That's very kind of you," I said. "But I don't mind introducing myself if you're busy. I don't expect you to babysit me."

"Babysit?" Mrs. Pankhurst raised an eyebrow. "Is that a quaint Americanism?"

I blushed hotly, something I seemed to be doing a lot of lately. "Um, yes, I guess so. I meant that you don't have to keep me company, I can manage on my own." I reminded myself that I'd met famous people before, so there was no reason to be nervous. Hadn't I talked to the painter, Edgar Degas, to the writer, Emile Zola? And the most important man for me to meet, Nigel de Grey, wasn't famous at all.

"Miss Lodge, may I introduce you to Herbert Wells." Mrs. Pankhurst led me to a middle-aged, portly man with a thick walrusy mustache who looked like Morton's brother. I was relieved I'd never heard of him. He didn't look at all impressive, even in his formal dress, more banker than writer. "He writes scientific romances, most ingenious stories."

"Scientific romances?" I asked, taking the hand offered to me in a damp handshake. "You mean stories about aliens and mechanical men falling in love?" I was proud I'd avoided the modern-sounding "robot."

"Hardly." Mr. Wells chuckled. "More like stories that stretch the imagination through science. Even if the science is not the kind taught in schools – yet, that is. I try to go beyond what we know today to what we'll know very well tomorrow."

"That sounds confusing," I said. At least it was for me.

"I'll give you a concrete example, that should help." Mr. Wells's eyes crinkled in a friendly way. He was obviously used to explaining this kind of thing. "Quoting one of my own characters, if I may, 'There is no difference between Time and any of the three dimensions of Space except that our consciousness moves along it.' Space and Time, you see, are a single entity. It's our perceptions that are limited. Scientific romances broaden our thinking. At least, that's my intention."

"Always on your soapbox, aren't you?" Mrs. Pankhurst laughed. "I'll leave the two of you to this fascinating discussion. I'm afraid space and time are confusing concepts for me, no matter how often you explain them. I'm a firm believer in the here and now."

"As am I!" Mr. Wells protested. "I'm simply also aware of the other possibilities around us."

"What do you mean by space and time being the same thing?" I asked. Was it a coincidence that Mrs. Pankhurst left me with this strange man? She couldn't possibly suspect I was a time traveler.

"I didn't say they were the same thing! I said they were part of the same thing – spacetime or timespace, whichever you prefer."

"You write about these things? I'd really like to read your books." If this man couldn't time travel himself, he might still have an explanation for the Touchstones and how they worked. I stared at him, searching for any signs that he was a time traveler, as if I could see cosmic dust on his shoes or a hazy glow from a Touchstone.

"The best known is probably *The War of the Worlds.* Or maybe *The Time Machine.*" His voice was low and gravelly, comforting somehow, so that I felt I knew him. Wait, I did know him – I'd heard of him after all!

"Herbert Wells? You mean H. G. Wells?" I must have turned bright pink. Again. So much for not being famous! "Of course, I know who you are!" *The War of the Worlds* was well known for the fake radio broadcast Orson Welles had made in the 1930s based on the book about Martians invading Earth. The radio show had seemed so real that many Americans had panicked, thinking Earth was actually being invaded by aliens. And *The Time Machine,* all that talk about spacetime and timespace! Did this prove H.G. Wells was a time traveler? If he was, wasn't he breaking an important Rule?

I wanted to ask him, but didn't know how without giving myself away. Instead I tried something else. "I think you know my mother." If he said yes, then he was definitely a time traveler. Though if he said no, maybe he was simply lying. "Her name is Serena Goldin."

Mr. Wells shook his head

thoughtfully. "No, I don't believe so. Is she also a writer? How would I know her?"

He didn't look like he was lying. But still. "Are you sure? She's a big fan of scientific romance."

Now Mr. Wells smiled. "I fancy myself a popular enough writer that I don't know each one of my admirers, though I'm delighted to hear that your mother is among them."

"I love your books too!" I gushed, trying to cover up the stupid mistake of thinking a writer would know all his readers. Wells probably just had a good imagination when he wrote about time travel. After all, in the book, he used a weird car contraption as a time machine, not Touchstones. He couldn't be a time traveler. That would be too big a coincidence.

Before I could ask him any more questions, a young man with slicked-back hair interrupted us, apologizing to me as he led Mr. Wells away to meet a reporter from the New York Post. If only I'd thought of that! I could be a young American cub reporter, why not? I scanned the crowd, trying to guess which people were writers, which were editors, which one might be Nigel de Grey.

A short, older woman with kind eyes set in a soft, friendly

face caught my attention. She was dressed plainly, like me, no fancy gloves, her only jewelry a simple cameo at her throat. She was probably a secretary, nobody important to talk to, but she was alone in the swirl of conversations, so I went up to her and introduced myself, trying on the junior reporter identity.

"Charmed to meet you, Miss Lodge. I'm one of Harold Warne's authors, Beatrix Potter," she said, inclining her head in a quick nod, her wispy hair threatening to fall out of its bun.

"Beatrix Potter!" And I'd thought she was a secretary. I blushed even hotter than when I'd met H. G. Wells. If only I control my face. "It's an honor to meet you! Your watercolors are perfect!"

Now it was her turn to blush – Beatrix Potter was blushing! "You're too kind. I fancy myself a plain little country mouse, and I always feel a bit awkward at these receptions."

"You're not awkward at all!" Look at me, I felt like saying.

"You say that because you're an American. You're free of the social standards we British bind ourselves to so tightly."

"I look American?" I laughed, wondering what that meant.

"Not look, my dear." Miss Potter smiled. "Sound. You sound American. You're a people I very much admire. Practical, that's what I'd call it. I'm a practical person myself, and I'm happiest puttering in my garden, taking care of my animals. Away from all this." She swept her arm out toward the chandeliers, the waiters carrying trays of champagne, the men in white ties, the women draped in jewels.

I nodded in agreement. "Not that I have a garden, or animals, but my life at home in America is nothing like this." That was the truest thing I'd said since I'd gotten to this time. "In fact, though I'm working as an assistant reporter, I want to be an artist too, and I sketch all the time." I rarely told anybody about my artistic ambitions or showed my drawings. I was too self-conscious, too critical, but Miss Potter made me feel comfortable. Maybe because she wasn't snooty, maybe because she dressed like a regular person, or maybe because her smile was so warm, her eyes so kind. "I wish I were as good as you! Peter Rabbit is my favorite, though I love Mrs. Tiggy-Winkle too. All your characters are wonderful!" Too late, I wondered if she'd written about the hedgehog character yet.

Miss Potter blushed again. "Good of you to say so. What do you like to draw?"

Phew! I hadn't slipped up by mentioning Mrs. Tiggy-Winkle, but I promised myself to be more careful in the future.

"I sketch what's around me, like people. For example, I drew you." Now I was the one blushing. What if she asked to look at the picture?

Which, of course, she did.

"I don't think I've ever been drawn before. Usually, I'm the one holding the pencil." She asked so sweetly, really, what could I do? I held out my sketchbook, equally miserable and embarrassed, a very uncomfortable combination.

"That's quite nice, isn't it?" She smiled at me. "You've made me pretty. Nobody's done that before!"

"You like it? Really?"

"Oh, yes! I'm impressed you can draw people! I only draw animals, you know. Somehow, I can capture them while humans completely elude me." She sighed. "I've always felt that creatures were my closest friends, which is why I find a room full of writers and publishing professionals so daunting. Generally, I avoid these things entirely, but I happened to be in London, so I agreed to put in a short appearance." Miss Potter took a watch out of her bag and checked the time. "And as soon as I can decently leave, I shall. Five more minutes should do it."

"I'm sure you could draw people if you wanted to. Your animals are so full of personality, they're practically human anyway!"

"That's not me. That's the animals themselves. I'll show you what I mean since I still have a few more minutes to fulfill my duty." Miss Potter took a small sketchbook out of the bag with the watch and led me to one of the floor-to-ceiling windows that looked out onto a formal garden. Bare-branched trees were evenly spaced in the square yard, interspersed with neatly manicured bushes, shaped into mounds as if scooped out like leafy ice cream.

It didn't look like a promising scene to draw at all, though I tried.

"It's not the garden that interests me, it's the animals," Miss Potter observed. "See that squirrel there, the one on that branch?" She quickly captured the animal in a few lines while I watched, amazed at the magic blossoming on the page. "Now you have a go."

I hadn't even noticed the squirrel before, the liveliest part of the view now that she'd pointed it out. My fingers felt clumsy and slow. Hers had danced so deftly over the paper and mine slogged, making heavy marks that looked more baboon-like than squirrelish.

Miss Potter took my notebook, examining my drawing, while I wanted to sink into the floor. She must have seen my agony, because she offered me her own sketchbook to look at, a sort of trade while she flipped through my pages.

And it worked, sort of. I was quickly lost in her adorable sketches, so full of life and energy. The animals almost walked off the page. I could see how smug the cat was, how kind the hedge-hog, how proud the mouse. All with the lightest of touches. How did she do it, turn a few marks into a look of curiosity, stubborn-ness, or vanity?

"You're quite talented, my dear, truly. You just need more practice. It's all about capturing the movement of the animal. Don't look at the edges, the outlines. Look at whatever gives the creature its character. That's what you need to capture." Miss Potter handed me back my notebook and took her own. "Now, tell me what brings you to London." She tucked her sketchbook back into her bag and smoothed the hair out of her eyes.

I couldn't blame her for changing the subject. I was fawning over her like a googly-eyed fan, which I was, truly I was, but I was here to do a job. Maybe she could even help me.

"I'm here to write about the publishing scene. Somebody suggested Nigel de Grey would be here and that he's had some in-teresting experiences with his authors."

"Nigel de Grey? He was with Heinemann, but I believe he's doing something for the war effort now, as so many of us are." Miss Potter looked around the room. "Oh, perhaps he is still an editor, because he's here, just as you said. He's the short, slender gentle-man over there, the clean-shaven one with the bushy eyebrows. You

know" – she lowered her voice conspiratorially – "I've always thought he was handsome. Don't you agree?"

I didn't, but I nodded anyway.

"Then I should go talk to him, shouldn't I?" I hesitated. I didn't want to leave her side. Part of me thought that if I stayed close to Miss Potter, Peter Rabbit would soon join us, then Jemima Puddle-Duck and Squirrel Nutkin. Or she'd let me look through her sketchbook again, which would be just as good.

"I suppose you should," Miss Potter said gently. "I wish you luck with your drawing. And your reporting story."

"Thank you, thank you so much." I curtsied awkwardly, which was probably exactly the wrong thing to do.

At least now I knew who Nigel was, I consoled myself as I made my way across the crowded room to the man Miss Potter had pointed out. He was sipping from a champagne glass while talking to a heavy-set man with an even more elaborate mustache than H. G. Wells had. This was clearly the decade for facial brushes.

"Pardon me," I said as I came up to the two men. "I'm sorry to interrupt, but I've been trying to find Mr. Nigel de Grey and I believe you're him."

"Indeed, I am." The shorter man, half the size of Mr. Mustache, smiled at me. He wasn't handsome and dashing like Miss Potter thought. He didn't seem like a genius code cracker, either, more like the kind of man who putters in the garden or builds elaborate model airplanes as a hobby. The kind of man you'd say would never hurt a fly.

"I'm a junior reporter from the Milwaukee Herald." I picked the most obscure city I could think of. "I was told you've had some interesting experiences that our subscribers would love to read about." I fingered the pages in my pocket. What excuse could I have for giving them to him? Or could I be a reverse pick-pocket, secretly stashing the papers in his pocket for him to find later.

"Who could have told you that?" Mr. de Grey seemed taken aback.

"A Mr. Morton," I said, naming Mom's friend, the Walrus man.

"Morton?" Mr. Mustache looked startled.

"But I don't know a Mr. Morton." Mr. de Grey wrinkled his brow, clearly puzzled. This wasn't working the way I'd meant it to.

"Fortunately, I do know this Mr. Morton," Mr. Mustache broke in. "Perhaps I can help you with your assignment. Let's discuss this matter with more privacy, shall we?" He pronounced it "priv-a-see" instead of "prive-a-see," so it took me a moment to understand what he was saying. Before I could protest, he took

my arm and steered me away, keeping a steely silence until he'd found a quiet corner where nobody could overhear us.

I was too stunned to struggle. Was he a Watcher?

I tried to stay calm. True, we were in a more out-of-the-way place, but we were still in a hall full of people. No way a Watcher would dare to grab me in such a public setting.

"What are you doing here, the truth now, if you please?" Mr. Mustache was firm, but hardly menacing.

"I'm sorry, I don't believe we've met. I'm Miss Lodge." I offered my hand innocently.

"Miss Lodge?" Mr. Mustache repeated the name as if it were the most ridiculous alias he'd ever heard. "Delighted to make your acquaintance. I'm Arthur Conan Doyle."

"Are you a writer?" I asked, wondering why he was so suspicious of me. "A journalist, perhaps?"

"A bit of both. You might have read my work. I'm Sir Arthur Conan Doyle." He enunciated slowly and clearly.

My mouth dropped open. You think that's just an expression, but when you're totally taken by surprise, that's exactly what happens. If I were a cartoon character, my eyes would have boinged out of my head. I stared at his face, searching for a resemblance to his famous detective. The nose was sharp, the eyes small and hooded with heavy lids, which made him look both secretive and piercing. Those two features were like Sherlock Holmes, but the rest of the ruddy face, the generous jowls, the ridiculous mustache, didn't fit at all.

"I'm very pleased to meet you," I stammered, though I didn't quite believe he really was the inventor of the greatest detective in literature. "I have to admit, you don't look like the way I imagined Sir Arthur Conan Doyle. I mean. . ."

"You mean, I don't look like Sherlock Holmes. No hatchet nose, no sharp chin or brooding brow. Nor am I tall and thin. I dare say I look more like your recent president, Teddy Roosevelt."

That was actually exactly what I meant. I guess that happened to him a lot, people expecting the writer to look like his character. And come to think of it, Beatrix Potter had a bunny-ish sort of aspect to her. Still, I was embarrassed to admit my disappointment. I did want Sir Arthur Conan Doyle to look like Sherlock Holmes and, better still, to think like him. Wait, maybe I didn't want that at all – that could be dangerous for me!

"My appearance isn't the point, however. Yours is. Why, I ask again, are you here? And how do you know Mr. Morton?" The face may have been round and jolly, but the eyes were sharp and shrewd.

"I'm here for a newspaper story." If he was as smart as Sherlock Holmes, could he tell by looking at my shoes that I'd hidden in the subway during a bombing raid, that I'd stolen a briefcase from a spy, that I'd come from the future? I nervously tucked the documents deeper into my pocket. Really, what could he tell by looking at me? "Mrs. Pankhurst invited me." I hoped her famous name would distract him.

Doyle leaned closer and lowered his voice. "I think you have entirely different intentions than those you claim. Your interest in Mr. de Grey suggests these plans have to do with Room 40, while your friendship with Mr. Morton suggests that you shouldn't be here at all." Doyle paused and said the next sentence with a piercing stare. "This isn't the right time for you."

I felt the blood rush out of my head, hammering loudly in my heart. Was Doyle saying I was a time traveler? Was he a Watcher after all? Would he grab me, here and now, in front of all these people? I wanted to run, but my feet were suddenly so heavy and numb, I couldn't move. I was frozen in panic.

"No need to be scared – you look as if I were about to skin you alive!" Doyle leaned back on his heels and smiled. "I just had to be sure. And now I am. So let's be honest with each other. Morton is a visitor from our future."

"A visitor?" I squeaked. Was he saying what I thought he was saying?

"Are you as well?" he pressed. "How do you know Morton?"

Were we really talking about this so openly? I looked around, mouth dry, but nobody paid us any attention at all.

"Morton's a friend of my mother," I admitted cautiously. If he was a Watcher, wouldn't he have hauled me off by now? He seemed almost amused. "And you haven't answered my question while I've answered yours – what do you mean by a visitor from the future?"

"I think you know precisely what I mean." Doyle gave me an icy stare. "Someone who can travel through time, skip through the centuries, meander through the millennia. Someone who knows how to use the Touchstones."

I shivered. He knew! Sir Arthur Conan Doyle, the author of the Sherlock Holmes mysteries, must be a time traveler!

So I made up my mind and took a big chance. "If you know about the Touchstones, if you know Morton, then perhaps you know my mother. Serena, Serena Goldin."

"You're Serena's daughter!" He relaxed now, looking genuinely delighted. Which meant he liked Mom. He didn't consider her a criminal or an enemy. My frantic pulse started to calm down. This could all be a good thing. Maybe Doyle could even help me.

"You know my mother? Can you tell me where she is? She wasn't hurt in the bombing raid last night, was she?"

"Fortunately, no bombs landed in London, and you're not allowed to see her, as you're perfectly well aware. You must know the Rules. Serena wouldn't allow you to travel otherwise." Doyle walked over to a passing waiter, helped himself to two glasses of champagne, and offered one to me. "You look like you could use something to steady your nerves."

"Thank you, but I'm too young to drink, and I'm fine anyway."

"Are you? Then what are you doing here?"

"Since you're so good at observation, perhaps you can tell me," I said.

"Ah, so you want me to play the Sherlock Holmes game, the parlor trick of telling you that you have an older brother, a father who's a photographer, that you live in California, and that you fancy yourself an artist."

How could he possibly know all that? Had Mom told him? How long had she been here?

"Naturally, you want me to reveal the decisive clues." Doyle smiled impishly, looking like a mischievous boy for a second rather than a middle-aged man. "The ink smudges on your fingers tell me that you've sketched recently. The fact that you used ink and not charcoal or pencil suggests you're a novice, not somebody who takes art seriously."

"That's not true!" I said hotly. "I draw in pencil as well as pen." I almost thrust my lumpy squirrel sketch, at him, but that would only make him think I was an even worse artist.

Doyle nodded. "That's one of the flaws of my method. I can notice the facts and draw logical conclusions, but leaping from there to assumptions of motive is always risky. A calculation that was worth a shot, however."

"What about everything else? There's no mark on my face

that tells you I have a brother, and while you can safely assume I have a father, how do you know he's a photographer?"

"Because your mother told me all this, of course!" Doyle roared with laughter.

"Well, I can safely make an observation about you, then," I said, annoyed that he'd played such a cheap trick, but also deeply relieved. "My mother must consider you a good friend or you wouldn't know those details. She's a very private person, probably even more so when she's . . . um, traveling."

"I'm honored that she considers me a friend. Your mother is quite exceptional, but then you already know that. I must confess, though, that I'm concerned about your mother now that you're here. That's not like her at all, to encourage you to travel. She's always said she'd wait until you were eighteen to tell you of your abilities. Why did she change her mind?" Doyle suddenly gasped, like he knew the answer to his own question. His brow furrowed with worry. "Tell me, what are you doing here? This isn't a touristic jaunt. There's a purpose, isn't there?"

Mom had planned to talk to me about this? I had so many questions, I wasn't sure which to ask first.

Across the room, Mrs. Pankhurst emerged from a cluster of people, now going up to talk to a short, slender man. The man kissed her hand and turned for the door, waiting for his cane and top hat. Suddenly I realized who it was.

"He's leaving! Nigel de Grey is leaving! I have to give him

something!" The servant was back now, with hat, cane, and coat. Another minute and Mr. de Grey would be out the door. I walked quickly in my long, awkward skirts, trying to keep a ladylike gait while hurrying past waiters with trays of champagne and hors d'oeuvres, clusters of people chatting.

A firm hand grabbed my elbow, yanking me back. "I must ask you to stop," Doyle whispered in my ear. "We need to talk first. You don't realize what you're doing."

"He needs these," I began. "I have something to give to Mr. de Grey, something that can save thousands of lives, maybe hundreds of thousands."

"Mira!" Doyle shocked me by using my real name. "You need to think before you do this. Please, I beg you."

"I know about the Rules, but this is the right thing to do!" I twisted away.

"Is it? Are you sure?" Doyle kept pace with me. "Do you know how you'll change the future? Aren't you playing with destiny here, with issues you can't possibly foresee?"

I stopped, my hand sweaty in my pocket as I firmly grasped the papers. Wasn't it a good thing to end a horrible war? Or was this something that was too big to change and whatever I did might actually make things worse?

It was too late anyway. Mr. de Grey was gone.

"Mira, I know you have questions. Unfortunately, this is neither the time nor place for such a discussion. I live in the country, but I keep some rooms in London. Please come see me there. Tonight. I'll explain everything. And I'll help you in any way I can." He handed me a business card with his name and address embossed in rich black ink.

"Not Baker Street," I noticed.

"Not Sherlock Holmes, either." Doyle offered a wry half-smile. "And now I must go. My public awaits."

As soon as he stepped away, three women dressed in swooshing gowns surrounded him, oohing and aahing over the brilliantly deductive mind of Sir Arthur. I fingered the card. Could he really be a time traveler? I would have guessed H. G. Wells was one. But ever since meeting Giordano Bruno in Rome, I'd been aware of the possibility that people I met in the past might be time travelers themselves. Though with Bruno, like myself, that had meant travels into the past. People like Sir Arthur Conan Doyle and H.G. Wells suggested travel also went the other way.

Which suddenly made a whole lot of sense. Mom must have traveled into the future too! That's where she saw the Horrible Thing, the disaster that would happen to us as a family, and that's why she was here now, in the past, trying to change things so that the future horror wouldn't happen. I'd assumed that one of her time traveling buddies had told her, someone like Morton, but Mom must have seen the Horrible Thing herself.

And now Sherlock Holmes, I mean his creator, Sir Arthur Conan Doyle, was offering to help me figure out the whole mystery! Who better to deduce the truth from the tiny bits of facts, the morsels of clues Mom had given me? I wished I could go to his house straightaway, but obviously he would still be here. I hoped the reception would end soon!

I scanned the room to see if I recognized any other famous people, though I wasn't sure I'd know them by sight. Mrs. Pankhurst held court over a group of young women, less ostentatiously dressed than the ladies who had thronged around Doyle. They looked up to her with pure admiration. H. G. Wells was in heated conversation with a young, balding man with glasses perched on his nose. Beatrix Potter had vanished, back to her beloved countryside, probably.

There wasn't much point to hanging around, asking editors about a position. That had been a lame excuse for Mrs. Pankhurst, not something I really needed to do. All I wanted now was to talk to Sir Arthur Conan Doyle. I could show him the papers in the briefcase, not just the few pages I'd managed to translate, but all of them!

I put down the glass of champagne I'd been holding all this time and snatched one of the toasts spread with black jam from a passing waiter's tray. I stuffed the whole thing into my mouth, but it wasn't jam at all! It was some vile fishy paste. Fish again! Was that all the British ate? I struggled to swallow it quickly so the taste wouldn't linger. Malcolm was right, the food was the worst thing about being here! It was definitely time to go.

I hated to interrupt the heated discussion Mrs. Pankhurst was having with her admirers, but I excused myself to let her know that I'd get home on my own, that she needn't introduce me to anybody since I'd talked to people myself. "Thank you so much for bringing me," I said. "I hope we can talk more back at the house."

"Of course," Mrs. Pankhurst said. "If you're sure you want to leave now. You could meet some fascinating young women, all ready to carry on the banner of our work." She smiled at the women, three of them with modern, short haircuts, all dressed sleekly in a totally different way than the fussy clothes of the older generation. And, of course, much more stylish than what I was wearing. They glared at me as if I had just gotten in their way, which I supposed I had.

"Another time, perhaps." I pasted on a fake smile. "I don't know why I'm so tired, but I'm truly exhausted. Good day, ladies!"

It felt good to be outside, not exactly in the fresh air since there was no such thing in London, but away from the stuffy, formal atmosphere of the hotel and its swanky guests. I wanted to go directly to Doyle's place, but first I needed to get the briefcase. I hadn't decided yet whether I'd show it to him, but I might, depending on what he told me. So I headed back to the house, asking for directions constantly.

The sun had set by the time I reached the tidy white row house. I rang the bell, rushed in, grabbed the briefcase, and headed right back out into the streets. According to the housemaid, Doyle's rooms weren't that far, a thirty-minute walk or so.

The house was behind the British Museum, so it was easy to find. Doyle probably wasn't home yet, but the museum might be fun to see in the meanwhile. This was one of the places on Malcolm's top-ten list. I figured I owed it to him to go inside. What if he was in the British Museum too, the exact same place, only a century later? Would he sense my presence? Would I feel his?

I was in luck. According to a sign outside, it was open late that night for a talk on Egyptian mummies. If I'd come here in

modern times, I would have had to check the briefcase, but now people just breezed in. There was no entry fee, so not even a line to buy tickets. Despite the fact that Mary Richardson had attacked a masterpiece with a butcher's knife, there were no security precautions except for the random guard pacing through the halls. Nobody stared at me as I carried the briefcase through the galleries, walking past famous objects like the Rosetta Stone and the enormous head of some ancient Egyptian pharaoh. The air vibrated with the past. In fact, it did more than pulse. The familiar magnetic pull tugged at me from all directions – I'd walked into a huge collection of Touchstones.

I should have known.

I couldn't tell if Malcolm or Dad were here in our present. All I could feel was the past. The Elgin marbles, taken from the Acropolis in Athens, mesmerized me. Waves of energy throbbed from the cool stones, calling me to touch them. I tried to hurry past, but was quickly pulled into their orbit. I was close enough to see the faint traces of color that had once covered the figures, close enough to see a purple haze shimmer from their stone skins. The horse's head on the end, the one surging out of the ground, was the hot, magnetic core of them all. I watched in horror as the ears flicked forward, the nostrils snorted, the eyes rolled wildly, all urging me to come nearer. The drapery on the figure at the other end started flapping, a cosmic wind whipping through the gallery.

No! I clenched my teeth. Not yet! I forced myself back, bracing against walls of heat. The briefcase was searing in my hand. I clutched it tighter, holding it against my chest as I forced my feet to move, inch by heavy inch, away from the stones. I struggled, determined not to give in – I couldn't go back, not yet. I had to get the briefcase where it belonged!

The air became lighter, clearer, until I could turn, wrench myself free of the sculptures' grip, and then it was over. I was out of the gallery, panting heavily, but free of their powerful hold.

I'd never been able to do that before, resist the pull of a Touchstone. I slumped down against the corridor wall, queasy and shaky, but I was still here, still in 1917 London. I got up on wobbly feet. Had anyone noticed anything? Luckily the rooms were empty. It was too late for most visitors. I started down the hall, my pulse slowly returning to normal, my steps firmer until I crossed another big gallery. I felt the familiar tug before I could see what was inside, the insistent pull to come closer, closer. I shuffled slowly on one foot, then the other. An ancient sculpture of a horse, a figure of a lion, two men in flowing robes, stood before a relief of sol-

diers battling. A plaque identified the group as coming from the Mausoleum at Halicarnassus, one of the Seven Wonders of the Ancient World.

I thought of Dad and his book on the modern wonders. I thought of Malcolm and how he needed me to be strong. I thought of Mom, hiding from the Watcher, trying hard to save us. I tried to focus on my family as the ancient statues drew me toward them, emitting their own eerie glow, a strange orangish light. I closed my eyes, forcing myself backward, slowly pulling myself out of the quicksand of time.

And then I was clear, back in the corridor, lighter and freer than before. I had to get away – the museum was a bad idea, a very bad idea. Touchstones pulled at me from every room. An Egyptian sarcophagus, a Greek urn, a Persian carving.

Except each time I resisted a Touchstone, I felt a surge of energy pulse through me. Each time was easier than the time before. Maybe I was becoming a better time traveler, as Morton had promised. I still couldn't direct exactly where or when I'd time travel to, but it seemed like now I could stop myself from going at all. That was huge improvement!

I tested my theory, coming close to enormous Assyrian winged beasts, but not touching them, walking past Cambodian gods without swerving closer. I could actually admire the incredible objects now without feeling too much pressure, just a dim hum-

ming in my breastbone. I was tempted to wander the halls longer, just to feel my growing strength, but Doyle would be home by now and I was eager to hear what he had to say.

My feet felt lighter as I walked out of the museum. Facing the Touchstones had been both exhausting and fortifying, like I'd put on time travel muscle, made myself stronger in some important way.

Full of this new confidence, I rang the bell of Doyle's house. A cliché of a butler, all thin lips, stern face, and jiggly jowls, led me into the study, a cozy, warm room after the cold, moonlit streets, comfortable despite all the strange objects scattered around. A skeleton hung in the corner, a violin was propped up near the sofa, books were piled everywhere along with interesting souvenirs, like a scale, a telescope, a collection of rocks and minerals, even a crystal ball like the kind used in séances. I bet his library would be fascinating to look at.

"Thank you for coming," Doyle greeted me, pouring the ever-present tea from a tray set on a low table between wingbacked chairs. "Please sit down. I know this can't be easy for you. Very confusing, I should think. Shall we start with the most basic issue — why are you here?"

I sank into one of the chairs, my head still throbbing from the vibrations of all the Touchstones. The weight of the briefcase in my lap reminded me of my mission, but I wasn't ready to talk about it yet.

"There's another issue that's much more basic to me." I took a sip of tea, braced by its sugary warmth. "Why was my mother waiting until I was eighteen? What was she planning to say then? And what changed her mind?"

Doyle sighed. "I really can't speak for your mother. I have children myself, so I certainly understand her desire to protect you."

"Protect me from what? From knowing the truth about her, about myself?"

Doyle leaned back in his chair. "Let's be logical about all this, shall we? Approach it like a Sherlock Holmes mystery. What are the facts?" He tented his fingers together, clearly relishing the game of playing his own character.

"The facts? I guess that there are people who can time travel, I don't know why. My mother is one of them. You're another. So am I. Can your children? Your wife?"

Doyle shook his head. "No, none of them. It's a rare gift. And a tremendous responsibility."

"Which brings us to the Rules, more facts. And to the Watchers, who are supposed to make sure the Rules are followed." I sighed. "All these facts don't amount to much."

"They give us a structure," Doyle said. "A way to understand this gift."

Exhaustion weighed me down, kept me from thinking clearly. I'd walked for hours and hadn't eaten anything since the awful fishy toast.

"Where are my manners? You need a good tea!" Doyle rang a bell by the side door.

"I have some tea, thank you." I leaned over the briefcase and took another sip.

"I mean tea, not tea," Doyle said, making no sense at all. "Marston will bring us some."

Marston was the angry-looking butler. He carried in an enormous tray with sandwiches, sliced meats, cake, and cookies (or biscuits, as the British say).

"Thank you, Marston, that will do." Doyle handed me a napkin.

"Tea?" I asked.

"Tea is also a meal, not just a drink, and I'll warrant you haven't had much to eat tonight." He offered me the plate of sandwiches.

"Thank you, I'd love one. Are there any fishy ones?" It would be too much to expect peanut butter.

"I believe there's chicken paste, cucumber, and there's probably salmon paste as well. Those will be the ones with pink filling, if you prefer fish."

Forewarned, I helped myself to several of the non-pink variety, added a generous slab of cake and some thin slices of meat. I liked the idea of tea as a meal. There wasn't all the silverware to worry about. Best of all, there was cake.

"Back to the facts," I said after I'd started on my first sandwich. "Does your family know you can time travel?"

"No, and I'd like to keep it that way, if you don't mind." Doyle nibbled on a pink-filled sandwich. It was tiny in his large hands.

"But isn't that too big a secret to keep? Aren't you gone for long stretches of time that you have to explain?" I was relieved that Dad and Malcolm shared my secret, that they helped me when I time traveled. Imagine lying in the present as well as in the past! The thought gave me a headache. Plus what a lonely life that would be, having only half-friendships the way I had with Clark. If that was even half a friendship. I wasn't sure what it was.

"I'm quite good at controlling when I leave and when I come back. I wasn't at first, of course, like you. So my first wife knew about the time travel. She died, however, and my present wife hasn't a clue."

"I'm sorry to hear about your first wife," I said lamely, not sure what you were supposed to say about a death in the family.

"It's an old wound. She's been gone over ten years now," Doyle said. "And I'm quite fortunate in my second wife. Anyway, spouses often know the truth for the very reason you say. It's hard to explain absences otherwise. That's why your father knows. But you were only meant to know once it was clear that you, too, had the gift."

I sat up straight. "It was clear? When? How?"

"I don't know the details. You must understand it's very rare, extraordinarily so, for a parent and child, for any two people in the same family, to be able to time travel. That's why the Rule about families and time travel was added only recently – well, what's recent to a time traveler, when all time is relative? It was only introduced after the danger became apparent, the increased risk that you could alter your family's future."

"Does it mean something, that both my mother and I have the gift?"

"Mean something?" Doyle helped himself to a slice of cake. "We're talking about facts, not interpretations. In any case, your mother knew somehow that you could also time travel, but she thought it would be too dangerous for you to actually travel until you were eighteen. Then she planned on telling you about Touchstones, the Rules, provide a sort of basic time travel tutorial for you."

"Time travel driver's ed," I said. "But she changed her mind. Why?"

"That's what I want to know. Did you find a Touchstone by accident?"

I thought of the first postcard we'd received from Mom after she went mysteriously missing. It had featured a gargoyle on Notre Dame cathedral in Paris, my first Touchstone. I shook my head.

"No, she led me right to it. She wanted me to time travel."

"Do you know why?" Doyle's tone was careful, precise. This was the most important question for him. And for me too, I supposed.

"She needed me to help her," I admitted.

"Help her how?"

"She wanted certain things done." I skirted the issue. I didn't dare say she wanted to change the future by changing the past.

Doyle sighed. "I was afraid of that. She saw something, didn't she? She saw something in the future, in your future, that was so dreadful, she decided to go back in time to keep it from happening. Except she needed you to go back too. Because you're the only one who can change your future."

Me? All this time, I thought I was helping Mom when really she was helping me? I thought this was about our family, or at least about Malcolm. Not just me.

"I understand you mother's impulse. I've even made the same mistake." Doyle stood up and started pacing, as if what he had to say was so awful, he couldn't sit still for it. "You'll do things for your children that you'd never do for yourself."

"But why not tell me the truth? Why all the mystery?" I

couldn't help it, I was mad. If this was about my future, she should tell me what was going on. Instead she was manipulating me!

"She wants to save you, not terrify you." Doyle sighed. "My own son, Kingsley, was badly wounded in this beastly war, the very first day of the Battle of the Somme last July. That was six months ago, and he's still recovering. When you see your child in agony, you'll do anything to stop it, anything, I tell you."

"What did you do?" I couldn't help feeling sorry for Doyle, but I was still sore at Mom.

"Like your mother, I thought I could use my gift, that I could travel into the past and prevent his destiny. So first I traveled into the future, to learn what could be done to make this war less deadly. I saw incredible inventions, undreamed of devices – aeroplanes that flashed through the air, bombs of devastating capabilities. But it's tricky, you see. I had to discover things that were possible in my own time, simply not yet imagined."

That was a different angle. Mom was trying to change things by setting off a series of reactions, like pushing down one domino so that the one far down the line will drop. It was a much less direct way of being effective. Although it didn't sound like Doyle's way had worked, either. I wondered if I'd be any better at figuring out solutions if I had more information. I'd been doing things blindfolded with Mom, not knowing all the facts, all the possibilities. Like what was the Horrible Thing in the first place and why did she think doing something here, now would make a difference? How did she pick the events to change?

"What did you find out that was useful?" I asked, hoping I could learn from Doyle's example.

"Things you would call, I believe, 'low-tech,' like body armor, life vests, and inflatable life boats. All simple enough devices that could save hundreds of thousands of lives. I wasn't just helping Kingsley, you see, I was helping all our British soldiers. I was doing my patriotic duty! And I saw clearly that this war would be won by the submarine and the airship, not by all our men in wretched trenches. I warned the government of the danger of a naval blockade. I told them we must build a channel tunnel to assure our route to Europe. But in the end all I did was make people think I was a crank. Except for Winston Churchill. He wrote me a nice little note."

"Maybe you did save your son. He might have been killed, but he was only wounded."

Doyle turned midpace and looked mournfully at me. "True, he wasn't killed, but he will still die. I saw that when I went into the future again."

My stomach sank. I could tell this story wouldn't have a happy ending. Maybe Doyle had only prolonged the inevitable, given his son a long, painful death instead of a quick, merciful one. Another reason why Mom should butt out of my future! She might actually be making things worse.

"He won't die from the battle. But there's another death

waiting for him. Next year, the Spanish influenza. There will be a devastating epidemic and many soldiers who survived the trenches will perish from the disease. A cruel trick of fate, don't you think? A way of Time proving she's always the winner, that nobody can manipulate her."

"I'm sorry about your son, but you used different methods than my mother. Maybe she'll be more successful than you. Not that I'm sure she should be. If this is all about me, I should have a whole lot more say in all this."

"Your 'say' should be to put a stop to it!" Doyle sounded angry himself now. "Nothing you do can possibly work for the simple reason that this isn't your time. You can't change things in a past where you don't belong. You can only make a real difference in your own time."

"But you were trying to change things in your own time. Why didn't that work for you?"

"Because I was trying to control my son's future, not my own."

"Are you saying change isn't possible?" I didn't believe him. Mom and I had already made a difference. We'd helped people on our way to changing whatever the Horrible Thing was. I had to admit, I'd cared more about fighting injustices than fixing some hazy not-yet-happened event. But that was the only way to get Mom home. Or was I wrong about that too?

"Let me be clear here. The key events of people's lives

can only properly be swayed by themselves – in their own present time. That's why you're playing with fire here. You may be changing something in your future life, but you can't predict exactly what that is, since you're so far from your actual time. You could end up setting off events that could be much worse than the ones you're trying to prevent!"

"How do you know that? Explain it to me." Where was that time travel tutorial I needed? Would Doyle give it to me now?

"You may make changes, all right, but they won't necessarily lead to the result you want. Imagine drawing a line straight out into infinity. Somewhere along the line, it gets bumped, nudged into another direc-

tion." Doyle stopped his pacing to quickly sketch something on some paper. "You may have wanted the line to go here, but it ends up here instead."

I thought of Giordano Bruno's binary trees, with time constantly splitting off. Doyle was basically saying the same thing.

"Do you see how the further you are from the event you want to influence, the harder it is to control that influence? It's like hitting a golf ball – it's much easier to sink a close putt than a long drive. The best way to change the future is in your own present, the time that's closest to your future."

Doyle handed me the paper, as if his drawing proved it. "Much as she wants to, your mother cannot protect you, just as I couldn't save Kingsley."

"If you know all this, why doesn't Mom? And since she knows I can time travel, why doesn't she trust me to take care of my own future?"

"Perhaps it's precisely because you can time travel that she thinks the two of you will succeed. There is a strange power to the family dynamic. And if she doesn't give you the details you crave, I'm sure it's to keep you safe."

Ignorance is bliss? Seemed more dangerous to me. But I got it. Mom was super careful about me doing anything on my own – from crossing the street by myself when I was tiny to taking the bus. She wouldn't let me take a plane by myself to visit Grandma in Los Angeles. No big surprise she wasn't going to let me wander on my own through the centuries. Except that's what I was doing, while following her cryptic messages. It's not like she was giving me much help.

The whole thing was stupid.

And I thought I'd been doing good. So did Malcolm and Dad. We were all helping Mom come home and saving the innocent along the way. Maybe that was still the best way to look at all this. Forget that she thought it was about me.

"Maybe I can help your son," I said. That wouldn't be stupid. "And all the British soldiers. Maybe that's my job, not yours."

"That's kind of you to say." Doyle slumped in his chair. "But you're missing the point. You haven't a job here. What is it you're trying to do anyway? You thought you'd tell Mr. Nigel de Grey where the U-boats are lurking? Or do you have some key to a German code you want to pass on to him?"

"Not exactly, but something like that." Did I trust him enough to tell him what we were doing? I wanted to. After all, he was a famous author, and being the creator of Sherlock Holmes automatically made him a good guy. Or made him seem like a good guy.

I thought about the facts he'd given me:

Sir Arthur Conan Doyle was a time traveler.

He knew my mother well enough to have heard about our family.

He'd also tried to change the past, so he'd dealt with the Watchers himself.

He was clearly very smart and was willing to tell me more about time travel than anyone else had.

Those all added up to good reasons to believe him. But what about Mom and her reasons? Here's what I knew about her:

Mom was a time traveler.

She had known I was also a time traveler. (How? What was the giveaway?)

Mom planned on teaching me about time travel when I turned eighteen, but she changed her mind. Again, why?

Dad thought she'd disappeared (and sent me in time after her) because of some Horrible Thing she'd seen in our future. Mom had suggested as much in notes she'd sent us.

We thought the Horrible Thing had to do with Malcolm and me, because she would only break the Rules for us, not for herself, the same as Doyle. But according to Doyle, she needed my help since only I could change my future, so the Horrible Thing only involved me. Or maybe me and her. Or maybe none of us and Mom was wrong about everything.

I sighed. It meant that not only was Mom using me by not being honest, she was being selfish. I thought we'd been noble, righting terrible wrongs, like people falsely accused of treason. But if all this was just about the vague future problems of me and Mom . . . it seemed far too risky to play with history this way, just like Doyle said. I mean, it was one thing if Mom and I could flip a switch in the past and – presto-chango – avoid some horrible car accident. But this was something else entirely. We were changing all of history just for us? That wasn't right. Malcolm and Dad would agree with me.

I took a deep breath, then patted the briefcase on my lap. "This is full of incriminating papers, proving the Germans have sabotaged American munitions yards, that they've attacked us on our own soil. If the United States government knew about this, President Wilson would have no choice but to declare war." I said it all in a rush, feeling lighter as the words flew out of my mouth.

Doyle stared in amazement. "How did you get that?"

"Does it matter?"

"Not really, but still." He rubbed his chin thoughtfully. "So this is why your mother is here, why you're here. It's tempting, it truly is, but are you sure that delivering those documents to the government is a good thing? Do you know precisely what the re-percussions will be from your actions?"

"It has to be a good thing, doesn't it? The sooner the United States joins the Allies, the sooner the war will end, which means fewer people will die." I hated to think Mom and I had been totally wrong. Well, really Mom was the one making the big mistake and I was just foolish for believing her. Except, I realized suddenly, she cleverly never told me exactly why I was supposed to do any-thing. She let all of us jump to conclusions, the way Malcolm had assumed Room 40 meant the Zimmerman Telegram. So while we thought this was about saving the lives of soldiers, maybe it had nothing to do with that. How could I ever trust Mom again?

"Maybe it's the opposite that should happen. What if the United States never enters the war? What if Germany wins?" Doyle shuddered. "Unpleasant though it is to say, perhaps that's what needs to happen."

"No! That's unthinkable!" My stomach churned sourly. Plus, it was too big a change. That couldn't be what Mom wanted!

"But I've seen the future. I know this isn't the war to end all wars that we think it is. If Germany weren't crushed, if it remained a strong power, became an even stronger one, would the Second

World War happen? Would millions of Jews die in the Holocaust?"

"Now you're the one playing with history," I argued. "My mother told me exactly the opposite, that you can't make big changes, only small ones." Could I believe that much? Had she told me anything that was true?

"What your mother doesn't want to admit is that small changes now can ripple into vast ones later. She's not looking far enough into the future to monitor the effects of her experiments. It's a dangerous business."

"But it's dangerous to keep America out of the war! If you follow your own logic, these papers need to get to Room 40. Forget what my mother wants – that's just common sense."

"Actually, if we followed rigorous logic, we'd return that briefcase to wherever you got it and let events follow their natural course." Doyle leaned over and patted my arm gently. It was an oddly comforting gesture. "The only safe way to change the future is when your actions, your decisions, are part of your own time. Your time created you, and you in turn should contribute to the direction in which it flows. That is part of who we are as self-determining beings."

"Are you saying that the Watcher is right to try to stop my mother?" That seemed to be the inescapable conclusion.

Doyle grimaced. "I hate to think of that fate for her."

"What fate?" The room was suddenly icy cold.

"You must already know how the Watchers work."

I did – people died because of them. Mom had outfoxed this one so far, but I was afraid for her. And Dad was terrified. He wanted Mom safely home, and I did too. Now more than ever.

"Let's say you're right," I said. "You're telling me I shouldn't help Mom. And maybe I actually agree with you. But I can't leave her here. I have to be sure she's safe!"

"Of course," Doyle agreed. "Serena needs to be with you in your right time. You'll have to convince her of that."

It would be easier to get into Room 40 than change Mom's mind about anything! And I still had the briefcase. "What am I supposed to do with this?" I asked.

"Let's see precisely what you have there." Doyle led me to a table and invited me to spread out the documents.

"They're in German. I managed to translate a few using a dictionary, enough to know how incriminating these papers are. See, this records payment to Lothar Witzke for blowing up a munitions factory at the Black Tom center in New Jersey."

"Hmmmm." Doyle put on glasses for a closer look. "There is nothing more deceptive than an obvious fact."

"Are you saying Witzke didn't sabotage the weapons before we could ship them to the Allies?"

"No, your translation is surprisingly accurate for someone who doesn't read German."

"What do you mean then?"

"I remember this fire. This happened last July. A fire started on Black Tom Pier, exploding the munitions there with such force that fifty people were killed, shrapnel pockmarked the Statue  of Liberty, and windows shattered as far away as Times Square. The police figured out pretty quickly that the fire was intentionally set."

"Did they catch the man, this Witzke guy?"

Doyle shook his head. "They never found out who was responsible. I don't think the Germans were even suspected. But this paper refers to an order to attack 'every kind of factory for supplying munitions of war.' These are orders from Captain Franz von Rintelen, a German naval officer who was based in New York. It appears from this that he contacted German sailors and officers living in New York and formed them into a sabotage crew, turning one of the German boats docked in New York harbor into a bomb factory. Very clever!"

"That's terrible! We have to tell someone!"

"He mentions a German-born chemist, now a naturalized American citizen living in New Jersey – a Dr. Scheele. This chemist made firebombs that were planted on Allied ships in American ports. Once at sea, the bombs detonated, setting off fires in the holds and destroying the arms being carried to the Allies. It all makes sense! Captain Rintelen was arrested here last August with incriminating documents. Perhaps copies of these very papers!"

"Are you saying these papers don't matter? That everyone already knows all this?" Did that mean there would be no explosion at Mare Island, that I didn't need to warn anybody? I was so confused!

Doyle sank back into his chair, suddenly looking tired and old. "I would say they matter very much. They're proof of the larger pattern of how the Germans operate. They aren't just trying to foster war between Mexico and America. They're supporting military dissension as distractions all over the globe. In England, that means helping the Irish in their demands for home rule. In Russia, aiding the Bolsheviks in their plot to overthrow the tsar. In North Africa, providing weapons for tribes to revolt against their colonial masters, the British. And in the United States, not just encouraging Mexico to invade, but Japan as well. They're creating a climate of fear so that America will be too worried about its own borders to look toward Europe. They want the Americans to think it's the Mexicans, the Japanese who are destroying their armaments, sabotaging their factories."

"So despite my mother – not because of her – I have to get these papers to Room 40, to the military authorities." I started packing up the briefcase. It was too late to go the Admiralty Building, but I'd try again in the morning. Now that I'd met Mr. de Grey, he'd recognize my name and let me in.

"I want to end this beastly war," Doyle said. "Besides my son, I've lost my brother, two brothers-in-law, and two nephews. But putting aside my personal feelings, is interfering like this the right thing to do?"

"It has to be! Anyway, the Zimmermann Telegram is supposed to push the United States to enter the war, so if that push comes a little sooner rather than later, how can that be a bad thing?" I was so angry at the Germans and their sneaky plots, I was ready to shove aside the guards at the Admiralty Building if I had to.

"Maybe it isn't, but who are we to make such tremendous decisions? One old man and a young girl?"

"There must be something I can do! I can't just throw these documents into the trash!"

"No, I suppose not. Who knows who may find them then. We have to make the best of a bad lot and get them someplace safe." Doyle started pacing again, then stopped with his back to me. "Give me the briefcase. I'll pass it on to the authorities. It's not right coming from you. You're not of this time." He turned to face me. "But I am."

I thought for a minute. Whether I agreed with Doyle or not about changing the past, it sounded like he'd take the briefcase where it could do some good. Mom thought I had to hand it over myself to affect my future, but I didn't care about that. I'd take care of myself in my own time, like Doyle said. The important thing now was to do the right thing for history. That meant helping to end a disastrous war. The rest didn't matter.

I had to trust Doyle. More than that, I had to trust myself.

I handed the case over without a word. It was as if a spark jolted from my hand, along the briefcase, up to Doyle's hand.

I hesitated, then asked, "And my mother? Do you know where she is?"

Doyle took a piece of stationery out of the desk drawer and wrote down an address.

"She goes by the name of Sara Langdon. She won't see you, but you need to get a message to her. Tell her the code crackers have the briefcase. Maybe that will be enough to get her home. If it isn't, you'll have to convince her that only you can change your fate, not her."

I folded the paper and stuck it in my notebook. "Thank you. For everything." He'd given me an incredible gift, a better understanding of what this was all about, even if that meant I couldn't agree with Mom anymore. I felt a twinge of guilt, but that was quickly swallowed by anger. And determination.

From now on, I'd be time traveling for a different reason. Not to change the future, but to change the present – to bring Mom back where she belonged.

Doyle walked me to the door and shook my hand. I wondered if I'd ever see him visiting twenty-first-century San Francisco. Or maybe I'd come back here as a tourist, just to catch up on old times. I smiled at the thought.

"Good luck," he said. "Now and in the future."

"I plan on making my own luck – and my own future."

January 18, 1917

Morton had said Mom was staying with the prime minister, which everyone knows would have put her at Number 10 Downing Street, not far from Big Ben. That wasn't what was written on the paper Doyle had given me. So which one of them had lied to me?

If Doyle was telling the truth, I would take that as a sign I'd made the right decision, giving him the briefcase. The next morning, back at Mrs. Pankhurst's breakfast table, I asked her if she recognized the address.

"King Charles Street?" She raised her eyebrows. "Do you have business with the government? The houses there all back onto Downing Street and belong to agencies of the prime minister."

So both Morton and Doyle were right! What a relief!

"Are you a secret suffragist after all?" Mrs. Pankhurst asked, pouring me some tea. "Plotting to break some windows on

Sylvia's behalf?"

"Of course not!" Had Sylvia actually done that? That would be like attacking the White House!

"No need to sound so surprised." Mrs. Pankhurst added some sugar to my cup. "She's learned her tactics from the best. We broke windows at Number 10 Downing when Lord Asquith was prime minister. He was such a brute! He actually feared we were planning to assassinate him. He was terrified of us 'little women.' That's what made him so cruel."

"Was he the one who passed the Cat and Mouse law?"

Mrs. Pankhurst smiled like a teacher whose difficult student has finally said something right. A look I knew all too well. "So you know something about the history of our protests after all. Yes, that act was his charming idea. One we used against him to defeat him

in the next election." She got up from the table and took a poster out of a drawer in the sideboard, unrolling it to show me. "I kept a copy because I was so proud of the image. Effective, don't you agree?"

"The new government is better, then?" It couldn't be worse, I supposed.

"Right now we're more

THE CAT AND MOUSE ACT

PASSED BY THE LIBERAL GOVERNMENT

THE LIBERAL CAT
ELECTORS VOTE AGAINST HIM!
KEEP THE LIBERAL OUT!

focused on the German threat. When the time comes, we shall renew our fight for suffrage, but for the present, we must all do our best to fight a common foe."

Suffrage was such a strange word to mean the right to vote. It sounded too close to suffering to be something good.

Mrs. Pankhurst put the poster back in its place and sat down again. "So I'd ask you not to cause any trouble for our present government. I'm working with the prime minister myself now and he's thinking of sending me to Russia."

"To Russia? Why?"

"There's fear a revolutionary government will take over, and if it does, it may pull out of the war. That would be a disaster for us. We simply can't allow it." Mrs. Pankhurst sighed. "This is another subject my daughter and I disagree about. Sylvia advocates for revolution in Russia. She wants a new socialist government to take care of the common people. But this isn't the right time for that. If only she had a bigger vision. If she saw how Germany is paying the Russian rebels, using them, she might change her mind."

Was that Mom, I wondered, blinkered by her own ideas, not able to see beyond her own small interests? I remembered what Doyle had said, that Germany worked not only to stir up war between Mexico and the United States, it encouraged the Irish to rebel against the British, and supported the Russian revolution. Talk about messing around with other people's destinies! The Germans were masters of it without bothering to time travel!

"Whatever happens in Russia, America will enter the war soon and that will change everything." I sounded more positive than I felt because I wanted so badly for it to be true.

"I sincerely hope so, but I'm not encouraged by your President Wilson. And he's been as nasty to suffragists there as Lord Asquith was to us here. Another reason women need to vote, so they can be sure the next president is better. He'd never have been reelected if women had a say!" Mrs. Pankhurst picked up the paper and squinted at Doyle's handwriting. "Now about that address. Why do you need to go there?"

"Not to throw stones, I assure you! Someone at the reception mentioned a possible secretarial position there, that's all. It's a live-in situation, so I wouldn't have to trouble you anymore." I figured I'd see Mom, or at least get a message to her, find a Touchstone, and get back to my right time. I might as well say good-bye now and give a convincing explanation of where I was going. Better than just rudely vanishing. I must have satisfied Mrs. Pankhurst's curiosity, because she sketched a map under the address.

London was a big city, but I seemed to be staying in the same small section of it. The map directed me past Convent Garden, where our hotel would be in the present. What would Dad and Malcolm be doing now? Would they be worried about me?

When I'd time traveled before, I'd gone back and forth a lot, thrust into the present by a Touchstone, then back into the past again without any planning or control. Now that I could resist the

Touchstones, I hadn't had the chance to check in with my support team. Malcolm would have done a lot of research for me, he would have been able to tell me what happened to Lothar Witzke, the saboteur, and where Mare Island was. He'd tell me if I should have given the briefcase to Doyle. I missed his help. And I missed Dad's encouragement. But maybe it was better this way. Cleaner, simpler. I'd just see this through, leave a message for Mom that this time travel stuff was over for me, I'd had enough of her manipulation, and find a Touchstone to get me back to present-day London.

Outside on the street, a vendor hawked his pies, a cart laden with bricks trundled by, a young girl in a pinafore held her nurse's hand tightly. A broad green awning tilted out from a row of stores advertising watches, bicycles, and flannel suits for 9 p 11, whatever that meant. I would miss seeing these kinds of things, history come to life. I was so focused on a man selling hot chestnuts, I didn't notice the woman walking toward me at first. But then I felt the air buzzing around me, the same anxious edge I'd felt by the stationery store. It was the Watcher, dressed in the same lilac felt cloak. Now I was close enough to see her sea green dress with lace trim, to count the pearl buttons on her shoes.

I started to run, looking for a store to dart into like last time, but she'd seen me. For wearing such a nice skirt, she could move surprisingly fast. Or my luck had run out. I tried to dodge her, panic filling my lungs, but she grabbed my arm.

"Let go!" I screamed. "Somebody help!" Where was a bobby – I mean, the police – when you needed one? Wouldn't a shop-keeper help me? A passerby? This was London, after all, not New York!

But nobody did anything. I guess a lovely young woman didn't seem like a real threat. Pretty smart for a Watcher to look the way she did. At least the German spy wasn't with her. That was the only thing that could have made this worse.

"I'm trying to help you," hissed the Watcher. "You have to leave! Now!"

"How can I when you're keeping me prisoner!" I yanked myself free and darted away. I couldn't let her catch me again. I zigzagged through the streets, dodging carts and cars, men carrying baskets of umbrellas, loaves of bread, large bolts of cloth, women lugging groceries, children, and piles of laundry. I must have lost her! Pretty good for someone not used to running in long, heavy skirts. But I didn't slow down yet, careening around a tight corner crowded with books set out for sale. And landed right smack in front of her perfectly pretty face.

The Watcher held me tighter than ever, by both arms now, like she was ready to shake me.

"I was leaving, like you said!" I growled. "It may shock you to know that I agree with you – my mom is totally wrong and she has to stop! That's what I'm trying to do now, convince her to give up and come home." It was true – she had to believe me!

The Watcher gaped, looking oddly like a goldfish, her mouth

open in a silent O. She slowly released me. She actually let me go.

"You're right. She's wrong." I rubbed my arms where her fingers had pressed so tightly, they'd left marks.

The Watcher narrowed her eyes, frowning. "You're going to help me? You finally understand what's at stake here?"

"I'm not sure how much I understand, but I do know that Mom needs to stop." I glared, daring her to call me a liar.

"Why should I believe you? This sounds like a trick."

"I'm telling you, I get it now," I insisted. "My mother can't change my future by changing the past. I know she thinks she can, by guiding me to make the change, but that won't work, either. The only way for me to change my future is in my own right time, in my present. So you can leave us alone!"

The Watcher's face relaxed. She was always coldly beautiful, but now she was pretty, her features warmed by a slow smile. "So the daughter is wiser than the mother. I'm impressed."

"My mother just wants to protect me and she's doing it the only way she knows how. It's hard for her to give up that control." As I said it, the truth of it struck me. Mom had to step back, to let go. My job should never have been to help her change my future. Instead, it was to show her that I could change my own, that I'd be okay without her.

"Will she listen to you?" The Watcher's voice was low and soft now. Which somehow made it all the more sinister, like a knife blade coated with honey.

"I don't know. I hope so." I was afraid Mom was too stubborn, too worried about me, to give up what she considered to be the only solution to the Horrible Thing. But I was even more afraid of the Watcher. I had to convince her to trust me.

"You understand now why I have to stop her, no matter what." The Watcher's voice took on the familiar steely edge. "And you should know, I'm not the only one."

We stood there, staring at each other silently for a long moment. Like we were dogs, sizing each other up. I didn't know what she saw, looking at me. Determination, I hoped. The courage to see things through.

Whatever it was, she must have believed me, because she didn't follow me when I started to walk away. She stood there, watching, like her name. When I looked over my shoulder after ten minutes of determined striding, she had disappeared. I kept glancing around to be sure I didn't lead her right to Mom.

Were Mom and I really on opposite sides now? My heart

ached, thinking about it. I wished I could stay mad at her, but I was too worried for that, too scared of the Watcher.

Chants erupted from somewhere to the right. I followed the noise to where the streets opened up in a big traffic circle. There, in the center, disrupting all the cars, trucks, and wagons, was a woman, surrounded by a crowd of other women. It was Sylvia, leading another protest.

This time there weren't men heckling them, but a ring of police officers was forming on the edges and an angry mood blackened the air.

"If we're not given the right to vote," Sylvia was yelling, "we'll take it – any way we can! We must be heard! With stones and bricks if not with words!"

"Stones and bricks!" the crowd echoed. Women pried cobblestones from the street, and they surged toward the buildings on either side, hurling stones at windows. The police ran forward, arresting some. But there were so many. Great panes of glass shattered with loud cracks and shards showered on passersby, who screamed and tried to dodge the splinters.

It was wrong, all wrong! This wasn't the way to earn the right to vote. I wanted to scream at everyone to stop it, but I was swept up in the shoving and pushing. A patch of blue surged towards me. Sure, no police around when you called them, but just when you didn't want to see them, there they were. Fear tightened my chest – I would be arrested! And what if the policemen were really Watchers? I darted through the crowd, using my small size to my advantage.

You read about crowds stampeding and crushing people under their heels. That's what this felt like, a wild mob gone crazy.

Police were grabbing women, wrenching them into wagons. Women were shrieking, throwing whatever they could get their hands on. Through it all, Sylvia still yelled her challenge.

"Stones or votes! Stones or votes!"

Then a louder crash than all the rest erupted and flames shot out of window.

A firebomb? People could be killed!

The crowd of women seemed stunned by the noise and fire. As more police drove up, the protestors dashed away, pouring down all the side streets. I ran with them, disgusted with myself for being part of something so ugly. But bigger than that was pure blind panic, inside and all around me, like a buzz throbbing through the air and in my bones.

We shoved our way through an alley, coming out into a clearing where a line of police, backed up by wagons and trucks, blocked the way. Women wailed and shrieked as they were pulled into the police wagons. Wildly searching for a clear escape, I ducked between two officers who were busy arresting protestors. I'd never even had detention, and here I was, dodging police for the second time in my life – both during time travel. This was wrong, all wrong!

A hand grabbed me. Another swung a stick at my knees. The crack of it stunned me with pain. I doubled over, crying.

"Into the truck, girly," the officer spat at me, shoving me into the back of a wagon already crammed full of women and girls. His eyes glinted evilly. Was he a Watcher? Or just a brute? Icy terror shot through me. How could I get away now?

I felt my leg carefully, probing for a broken bone. Despite the searing ache, I was only bruised. I could see blood pouring from a gash on one woman's head. Another cradled a broken arm. I tried to feel lucky, but all I felt was dread.

The truck's engine rumbled to life and we were thrown forward as it lurched down the street.

"Where are they taking us?" I asked the girl next to me.

"Where do you think?" she snapped. "Prison."

Mrs. Pankhurst's horror stories ran through my head, adding to my memories of the Roman dungeon. I couldn't face prison again, I just couldn't!

I braced myself as the truck careened around a corner. None of us were handcuffed. Maybe that would be all the freedom I needed to escape. I tried to open the back door, figuring we were going slowly enough, it was worth risking a jump, but the door wouldn't budge from the inside. I'd have to wait until we stopped, then take any chance I could get. Anything was better than jail!

A quavering voice somewhere toward the front started to sing, a chant to give us courage. I didn't know the song, but more women joined in, lifting all our spirits, until the whole wagon echoed with the brave melody. I didn't know the words or tune to sing along, but the melody surged through me, pushing away the fear. I could do it, I knew I could. I'd get out somehow!

When the truck finally stopped, the women kept on singing.

An officer opened the back with a clang.

"Out you go," he ordered. "Line up there and into the station. That's right."

The women filed out, still singing. They followed the policemen leading the way, defiant, but obedient. Except for me. I wasn't going to make it so easy for them. There were only three officers. This was my chance.

I jumped down from the wagon, testing my leg. It was sore, but I could walk. I took a quick step. And another. Away from the station, from the line of women.

"You, there!" a policeman bellowed.

I didn't turn around to see who he meant. I bolted, running on my injured leg as well as I could.

"Stop!" another policeman yelled, charging toward me. All around me now, women were running. The meek, obedient line wasn't obedient any more. There was no more singing, just the rasping of heavy breathing as we all scattered in every direction, far too many to all be caught.

I'd become an expert on running through London streets, figuring out which narrow alleys held the most promise, which crowded roundabouts offered the most confusion. I ran with tears running down my face, pain wrenching my leg, fear clutching my throat. I just wanted to go home, to see Dad and Malcolm. I whipped past a statue in a park. It was probably a Touchstone – I could be safely gone now!

But I kept on running, because I had to see Mom first. I had to convince her that I was right and she had to come home.

A wave of homesickness threatened to swallow me up. I just wanted to be a normal girl, back at home with my friends, dealing with normal problems like worrying about tests and who likes who. What could I say so Mom would see how stupid and pointless all this was?

I had thought Sylvia was brave, but maybe she was simply foolish. And Mom was being shortsighted in the same way. It was all so confusing, figuring out what was right and what was wrong. All I could do was trust my instincts. That old saying, the ends justify the means – Mom and Sylvia clearly believed it. But I didn't. How you did something was just as important as what you were doing. Getting the vote didn't make destroying property right. And trying to save your kids didn't justify changing history, especially when you couldn't be sure what would be the result of your changes.

If I couldn't convince Mom, we might end up like the Pankhursts, a family divided by a huge chasm. That was the something I had to prevent, a truly Horrible Thing for all of us.

The streets grew more crowded, making me feel safer. I limped awkwardly now, allowing myself to favor my bruised leg. I searched for street signs to give me a sense of where I was. It looked like I was near a train station. Yes, a large sign marked Charing Cross Station. I knew that name – if I remembered right, I wasn't far from Downing Street.

Rows of soldiers marched towards the trains, probably

on their way to the trenches in France. Carts and wagons with crosses painted on them went the other direction, carrying the wounded away from the station.

As I came closer to the station itself, I saw clusters of soldiers on stretchers or sitting on crates, some bandaged and bleeding. These were soldiers returning from France. The lucky ones were haggard and filthy. The others stared blindly into space, shell-shocked, or bloody, or both. I've seen my share of gore in movies, but this was something else. The smell alone was sickening. I tried not to look, to focus on my leg, which felt healthy in comparison. I couldn't bear to see the gaping wounds, the holes where ears and noses had been.

Beside the nurses, women volunteers had set up tea trolleys and were handing around cups of tea and plates of cookies. I had to admire them – I couldn't face those terrible injuries, the howls and moans of pain. I just wanted to get by as quickly as possible.

I recognized Mrs. Pankhurst, bending over a soldier with gauze thickly wrapped around his head. She hadn't mentioned she was coming here, but I knew she did a lot of work for the war, so I wasn't surprised. She was truly impressive, giving her life to one important cause after another, without a hint of selfishness. If only Sylvia could see things from her mother's point of view!

If only Mom could see things from mine! I couldn't tell her she was actually being selfish, but I could say the obvious, that real lives were at stake. I had to convince her to stop trying to control our fate. If she really cared about Malcolm and me, she'd be our mother now, right now, today. And she'd trust us to guide our own futures.

I edged my way through the soldiers, trying not to stare at a man whose face was entirely wrapped in bandages so he looked like a cartoon mummy. Anything I could do to shorten this misery had to be right. Or was I fooling myself? Imagining myself to be some kind of knight in shining armor when I was actually part of the problem. Maybe instead of telling Mom what to do, we could talk about it together, figure out our choices as the team I wanted us to be.

I asked one of the nurses if she knew King Charles Street. It was even closer than I thought and before I was ready, I found

myself in front of a brick house with green-painted eaves. Mom was somewhere inside. Was I ready to face her? Would we have a real discussion? Or would she run away before I had a chance to say anything?

I hesitated. She would run away, the way she'd done every other time I'd glimpsed her in the past. The only way to talk to her would be to trick her. Which meant I had to disguise myself. But how?

I thought of the soldiers I'd just walked past, disfigured by bandages. That was it! I rushed back to the train station. Scanning the crowd, I found a nurse wrapping a soldier's arm in long swaths of linen. Edgy with nerves, I hurried up to her.

"Miss, I'm sorry to bother you, but my brother's been wounded. Could you please give me some of those bandages to stanch the bleeding? There are so many hurt men, too many for you nurses, and I can help out." I felt terrible lying about something like that, ashamed to take medical supplies away from men who truly needed them, but this was the only thing I could think of to use as a disguise.

"Of course, here, take this," the nurse said, not even look-

ing at me, she was so intent on her patient. I took the offered strips, as few as possible, reassured myself that she had plenty, mumbled a quick thank you, and hurried away. As soon as I'd turned the corner and put the station behind me, I ducked into an alley and wrapped my face as well as I could, covering the bottom half awkwardly, but enough so it would be difficult to recognize me.

Looking like a partial mummy, I knocked on Mom's door. I assumed a maid or butler would open it, but when the door swung open, there stood Mom herself. Her curly hair was pinned back into a loose bun and she looked slighter, smaller, in the high-necked gray dress with a thin shawl draped over her shoulders. Her face was drawn, tired, and sad. I wanted to throw my arms around her, to tell her I missed her, I loved her. I wanted to beg her to come home.

But that would only frighten her away. So I kept my hands at my side, my heart pounding wildly. Was she sad because she missed us? She had to be lonely, stuck in the past without us. Another good reason to stop all this.

"Yes?" she asked. So my disguise worked.

"Sara Langdon?" I rasped, my throat dry.

"Yes, I'm Sara Langdon. And you are?" Mom leaned closer, searching what she could see of my face.

"I need to speak with you. It's urgent. About your daughter. And your son." I bowed my head so she couldn't see much and pushed my way past her, into the house. Please, Mom, I thought, listen to me, please!

"How do you know my children?" Mom demanded. "Who are you?"

"Listen to me, we don't have much time. You have to listen to me!" This time I said the words out loud.

"I don't have to do any such thing!" For a minute, I thought Mom might slap me.

"You can't change your children's future by messing with the past. They're the only ones who can, by the choices they make, the actions they take – in their own right time. Your family needs you with them now, not far away in the past where you can't help them. And you may instead harm a lot of innocent people."

"I'll ask you one last time, who are you? You're not a Watcher, are you?" Mom grabbed at the bandage around my face and yanked it off.

"Mira!" Her face went white.

"Mom, listen to me! You have to stop this! I'm not doing this for you anymore. And you can't change things without me, so you should just quit. I'm begging you!" I grabbed her hand. She felt so familiar. She smelled like home!

"Oh, Mira, no, you can't be here!" Mom yanked her wrist back, her voice tearful. "No!" she sobbed and turned to run down the front hall, a narrow passage with striped wallpaper hemming us in even more.

I limped after her, my leg aching from the blow and all the

running I'd forced it to do. "You follow that Rule because you know it's important, but all the Rules are important, especially not changing anything. You can't help me, Mom, not this way! And you're just being selfish!"

Mom ran through a kitchen, startling a cook and two maids, and hurtled out the back door, yelling furiously. "My own daughter doesn't believe me! You've betrayed me, you!"

That wasn't true – I loved her, I was trying to help her! She was the one who didn't believe me. This was the closest I'd been to her in ages, but we were farther apart than ever.

"Mom, please!" I wailed. "I love you!" Maybe that would make her stop and listen, but she didn't falter, didn't hesitate, just dashed into the back garden. "Mom, you have to trust me! This is about my future!"

Mom turned to face me, tears streaking her cheeks. "Yes, your future, and I'll make sure you have one!" I thought she'd changed her mind, that she was coming toward me, that in another minute, she'd be hugging me and telling me how much she loved me. Instead, she reached out and touched a small fountain in the center of the yard. Blue-green light crackled around her and then she was gone, the light wavering and sputtering like the last sparks of a firecracker. The fountain had to be a Touchstone. The question was when she'd gone to.

I stood there, dazed, hollowed out with sadness. Why couldn't she listen to me? Why couldn't she trust me to keep myself safe? Why couldn't she admit that maybe, just maybe she was wrong and I was right?

I wasn't sure what to do or where to go. But there was the fountain in front of me, a Touchstone calling to me. There was nothing left for me to do here. All I wanted was to see Dad and Malcolm, to give them both a big hug. I stretched out a finger, closed my eyes, and touched the cold stone.

Winds swirled, explosions echoed distantly, lights crackled and whipped around me at dizzying speed. When the world settled down, I was still in the garden, though now it was overgrown with weeds. From the satellite dishes on the homes around me, the airplane soaring overhead, the smell of the air, free of coal and soot, I had to be back in the present.

I'd lost Mom, but I still had Dad and Malcolm and I needed them more than ever. Somehow being here, in the right time, made my bruised leg feel better, stronger. Running might not be a good idea, but at least I could walk on it.

I knew the name of the hotel we were staying at, so I headed there. Like every place I'd been to so far, it was a long way to go, but manageable. The streets were the same as in 1917, but most of the buildings were completely changed. I recognized Big Ben, the Houses of Parliament, and the river alongside them. But the water wasn't full of small rickety boats now. There were no shanties along the shore. The city felt clean and brisk and efficient, like I was walking inside a giant mechanical clock where all the pieces fit together perfectly. London had been a messy patchwork of neighborhoods before. Now I saw the same shops that sprouted up all over the world, the ever-present McDonalds and Starbucks, but also Office Depot and Cold Stone.

I was back in my jeans and T-shirt, my comfortable shoes. I took a deep breath and couldn't help grinning, even with all the depressingly modern places around me. This was when I belonged, and as I walked, the sadness seeped out of me, replaced with the sense of being in the right place at the right time, a world where women could vote and work and even be prime minister.

As I got close, I saw them, sitting outside at a café near the hotel. Malcolm was doing something on his phone, probably using the free Wi-Fi to do research for me, while Dad solved one of his crossword puzzles. A warm rush of love filled my chest. That was so Malcolm, so Dad!

And then I saw someone else I knew and fear soured the pit of my stomach, filled my mouth with a chalky dread.

It was the Watcher.

Yes, it was definitely her. Her hair was cut short and she looked stylish in a sleek skirt and high heels. As I watched in frozen horror, she click-clacked closer to Malcolm, leaning over to say something to him.

"Dad! Malcolm" I yelled, running frantically, my leg throbbing.

Malcolm turned to gape at me. Dad bounded up from his chair.

"Don't trust her!" I shrieked. "She's the Watcher!"

Malcolm was fast – he grabbed the elegant woman's wrist. "Where's my mother? What have you done with her?"

"Malcolm!" Dad yelped. "Let her go!"

"No, this is our chance to get some answers." Malcolm forced the Watcher into his chair, standing over her as if he were a hulk, not a skinny teenager. But he was strong, I'll give him that. And determined. Dad looked ready to have a heart attack, as if he thought Malcolm was being the bad guy, assaulting a lady.

"What are you doing here?" I demanded, grabbing her other wrist. "Malcolm's right, it's our turn for answers."

The Watcher didn't struggle. She sat back serenely in the chair. "Do you really think you can hurt me? That you can do anything to me? You're the ones breaking the Rules and you'd better stop."

"Or what?" Dad thundered. He was on our side now, not taken in by the Watcher's pretty face.

"Or we'll send you where you can't trouble anybody anymore. Mira knows what I mean, don't you, dear? She's admitted that your wife is making an enormous mistake. So why don't you all open your eyes and do the right thing? It'll be better for everyone that way, including Serena."

"Don't you hurt her!" Malcolm twisted her wrist. "And leave my sister alone!"

The Watcher blinked slowly, like some kind of poisonous snake. "I think your sister can take care of herself. And so can I."

I tried to hold on and I'm sure Malcolm did too, but she calmly stood up, flinging off our grips like so much dust. "Now do the right thing or the next time, I won't be so nice." She clacked away on her stilettos, stabbing the sidewalk. "You know where Serena is. It's your job to bring her home. Now."

Malcolm lunged after her, but Dad pulled him back. "Let her go. She's not telling us anything. She just wants to scare us."

"What did she mean that Mom's making a mistake? That you said so?" Malcolm looked at me as if I'd betrayed him.

"Let me explain."

Before I could say anything else, Dad folded me up in a hug. "I'm glad you're safe. That's what matters most. That Watcher is scary."

"Yeah." Malcolm nodded. "You know, it didn't seem real before, where you went, what you did. But seeing her, that brought it home. This is all way more complicated than we thought."

He had no idea.

"Sit down, Mira, eat something," Dad said. "Where were you? What happened?"

I sank into a chair, suddenly exhausted. "First, you tell me how long I've been gone."

"Not too long, a couple of hours. But long enough that we had lunch without you." Malcolm gestured to the empty plates on the table and sat down himself – not in the chair where the Watcher had been, I noticed.

"Are you hungry? I'll get you a menu." I knew Dad was eager to hear about Mom. I gave him credit that he could even think about ordering food. It was one way he knew how to take care of me.

"I'm fine. I ate a century or so ago. You were right, Malcolm, it was about the Zimmermann Telegram, about German plots. I was in London, January 1917. And I not only saw Mom, I talked to her!"

Malcolm and Dad were way better than I was with Doyle, not interrupting once as I told the whole, long story. When I was finished, there was a thick silence. Malcolm looked like he was solving a complicated equation in his head, as if maybe what I'd said didn't add up. Dad looked stunned. Was he mad at me? Did he think I'd betrayed Mom the way she did?

"We've got to rethink everything." Malcolm said slowly. "Decide what we should do now. And in the past. I wish we understood time travel better. And how the Watchers work."

"Are you angry?" I asked, afraid to hear the answer.

"At you? You didn't do anything wrong! And I'm impressed – you're getting really good at all this stuff." Malcolm reassured me. "And you got to meet H. G. Wells, Beatrix Potter, and Sir Arthur Conan Doyle! You are SO lucky! Please, promise me when you go back, you'll get his autograph. That's the least you can do for me."

"You know I can't bring anything back from the past." I searched Dad's face, but I couldn't tell what he was thinking. He just looked sad. And more worried than ever.

"Have him sign your notebook, that always travels with you." Malcolm was like a dog with a bone. There was no way to make him give up until I agreed.

I fingered the book in my pocket. "Yes, I guess I could, but I wasn't planning on going back."

"I'm so sorry that you've had to take these risks," Dad said quietly. "Everything's changed now. We were working together as a family, but we didn't understand what we were doing. I have to admit, your mother never explained time travel to me the way Arthur Conan Doyle did to you. I just believed her. We all did." Dad leaned forward and touched my shoulder. "It's not her fault, you know. She's not intentionally doing the wrong thing. She's doing all this to save you, at least that's what she thinks."

"I know." I knew that better than anyone. "She may have the right reasons, but she's doing all the wrong things."

"So now we have to save her. You have to make her listen to you. Get Morton on your side. Ask Arthur Conan Doyle to talk to her." Dad looked equal parts desperate and frustrated. "We've seen how serious that Watcher is. We can't let her get to Mom."

"So you're not mad at me?"

"Of course not, Mira! You've been so brave in all of this, willing to do whatever Mom said was necessary." Dad ran his fingers through his hair, as if he was trying to erase all the fears stored in his forehead. "In some ways, this is a huge relief. The Rules are right and we should follow them – Mom should follow them. Even if the Watcher seems wrong."

"But what about the Horrible Thing we're supposed to stop from happening? Won't something bad happen to Mira in the future now?" Malcolm asked. "Do we believe Doyle and leave you to take care of yourself?"

"Yes! I'm not a baby. Anyway, the only way to change my future is for me to do it, in my own time." I explained the time lines and binary trees that Doyle had outlined. "Now that I know to be careful, I'm sure I'll be able to figure out what it is I need to do."

"Maybe, but I'm still going to help you. In the present, if not in the past anymore." Was I imagining it, or did my brother look worried?

"We all will," Dad agreed.

"Anyway, we don't need to worry about my future now. We need to get Mom home. Except I don't know how to convince her." I slumped in my chair. "That's an even bigger job than anything she's asked me to do."

"Here's the thing about Mom," Malcolm explained. "She's completely logical. If you lay things out for her clearly and rationally, you can always get her on your side. That's worked for me whenever I've asked her for anything. Since I was three years old."

"But if you're emotional, you'll lose her," Dad added. "You can't appeal to feelings or morality, what's right and wrong, because those are all gray areas, open to interpretation."

"Morality is subjective?" I completely disagreed. It was always wrong to kill somebody. Though I could agree that sometimes lies – little white lies – were better than an ugly truth.

"Of course it is!" Dad argued. "We as a society agree that certain things are wrong, but those same things may not have been considered bad years ago or might not be in the future. Or maybe thought okay right now by other societies. Take polygamy or cannibalism. Those are wrong to us now, but not every human throughout time has thought so."

"You're the time traveler – look at history," Malcolm added. "Women couldn't vote in 1917, right? Because people thought they weren't competent, that they couldn't make intelligent political decisions."

"By people, you mean men," I countered. "That's not morality, that's prejudice, plain and simple."

"There were conservative women too, women who agreed with their menfolk. Anyway, you get the point. People argued it would be morally wrong for society if women voted, didn't they?"

"I guess," I admitted. Was that really about morality or about holding onto power?

"You guys are getting off topic," Dad said impatiently. "Seriously, Mira, think of this from Mom's point of view. You can't convince her something's right or wrong. But you can prove to her that what she wants to do isn't possible. Like Arthur Conan Doyle said, only you and Malcolm can truly affect your futures."

"But how do I prove that to her?" It wasn't like I could turn that proposition into a mathematical formula, a bit of computer coding that Mom could read.

If x, then y. If y then z.
So, if x, then z.

"Maybe you can't, but surely the king of logical thinking can!" Malcolm grinned triumphantly.

"You mean Arthur Conan Doyle?" I was doubtful he'd do anything else for me.

"If the creator of Sherlock Holmes, with his ruthless, impeccable logic, can't convince Mom, then who can? You've got to go back, not to see Mom, but to see Doyle."

"Do you agree, Dad?" I asked. "After all, Doyle already knows that Mom is wrong. He's the one who explained it all to me, and he's had plenty of chances to talk to Mom. They're friends!"

"But he doesn't know Mom well," Dad said. "He thought Mom would listen to you because you're her daughter, because you're asking her to leave your future in your own hands, where it belongs, but that's an emotional plea."

I kind of got it. I thought Mom was cold sometimes, but really she was coolly logical.

"Look, Mira, you've gotten so much better at time travel," Malcolm said. "You weren't sucked into touching Touchstones when you weren't ready, and when you wanted to come home to us, you did, right away. That wasn't true when you time traveled before.

So this will be easy. You go back, talk to Doyle, you come home."

He made it sound like a trip to the store to pick up some milk. What if there was a zeppelin attack exactly when I got there? What if the German spy saw me and recognized me as the girl who snatched his briefcase? What about the Watcher?

Dad saw my hesitation. He reached across the table and took my hand. "I'd trade places with you in a heartbeat, you know that. But how else can we get Mom back? What choice do we have?"

I squeezed his hand. "I guess I'm the only one who can fix this." If Dad or Malcolm could time travel, they'd be there by now themselves, happily having tea with Arthur Conan Doyle. "Okay, I'll try." Because really, that was the moral thing to do (yes, Dad, there was such a thing as morality). "But you have to be careful yourselves, now that you know what the Watcher looks like. At least this one – there are others, remember."

"Don't worry about us. Just take care of yourself. You'll get Mom home, I'm sure of it." Dad smiled. I hoped I could live up to his faith in me, but really this all depended on Mom much more than on me.

"So shall we take a walk, look for a Touchstone?" Malcolm suggested, eager to get going.

While Dad went inside the café to pay for their lunch, Malcolm flipped through his phone.

"Do you want to know what I learned while you were gone? What I was researching?"

"Does any of it matter? Is there something I need to tell Doyle?" I got out my sketchbook, ready to take notes.

"Hmmm, maybe not. I didn't know you were going to meet him, so I wasn't reading about him. Let me see what I can find out now. . . ."

"Let me guess. He wrote to Winston Churchill and advised him to equip boats with life vests and inflatable life boats, plus body armor to protect the soldiers in the trenches. Crazy, futuristic ideas like that!" I started drawing the scene around me. The other people sitting outside, the signboard advertising daily specials. If I practiced more, I'd get better, like Beatrix Potter said.

"Actually, yes. At least he wrote to the War Office with those suggestions after the navy lost over a thousand men at sea in a single day, but everybody thought he was ridiculous. Except Winston Churchill, who thanked him for the ideas." Malcolm scrolled down the screen.

"He admitted he got those ideas from time travel. That was one of the examples he gave that trying to change history doesn't work. He hoped one of those devices could save his son's life."

"Which would be a selfish kind of use for them, but it sounds like Doyle was a staunch patriot and a big supporter of the war." Malcolm continued reading from his phone. "He even tried to enlist, though obviously he was too old. So instead, he organized a volunteer battalion of civilians to help on the home front. He went to the front himself in 1916 as a writer, since he couldn't go as a soldier, doing research for a book called *The British Campaign in France and Flanders*. It sounds like he saw the worst of trench warfare."

"He didn't mention the book, or trying to enlist, or going to the trenches. He didn't tell me that he'd seen the fighting up close. He sure didn't act like a hero." A woman at a nearby table had a dog with her. I tried to capture him the way the squirrel had emerged

from Miss Potter's quick lines.

"I don't know about being a hero, but he did what he could. He even used Sherlock Holmes for anti-German propaganda."

That surprised me. I stopped drawing and stared at my brother. "I thought he'd killed his character off long before the war started. Wasn't that a huge story? People were so upset that Holmes had died, it was as if they were mourning a real celebrity, not a fictional character."

"You're right, he had Holmes killed at the hands of his archenemy, Moriarty, long before the war. It says here that by 1893, Doyle had resolved to kill Holmes – 'even if I buried my bank account with him,' he wrote in his autobiography. He set the scene at Reichenbach Falls, an Alpine cascade in Switzerland. Doyle's editors despaired, but the author felt only relief: 'I have been much blamed for doing that gentleman to death, but I hold that it was not murder, but justifiable homicide in self-defense, since, if I had not killed him, he would certainly have killed me.' Wow! What did he have against his own character?"

"We didn't talk about Sherlock Holmes at all, so I have no idea. Though I can guess he felt like his life was being taken over by Holmes. Anyway, he clearly didn't leave Holmes a ghost if he was writing about him after 1914."

"He brought him back long before the war, actually, starting in 1902 with *The Hound of the Baskervilles,* though he cheated and said that adventure happened before Holmes's untimely fall to his death. The next year, he wrote that Holmes had faked his death, which allowed for dozens more stories, plus four novels, including *His Last Bow,* where Holmes infiltrates and captures a German spy ring, much like the one you found mentioned in that briefcase."

My mouth turned dry. "What did you say? Did Doyle use those documents for a story? Didn't he give them to the British government, to Room 40? Quick, Malcolm, find out when that story was written!" I hoped he'd say 1915 or '16, before I'd met up with Doyle although as a time traveler, he could easily take the information I'd given him, hop back a year or two, write his story, then return to his present. But that would be wrong, so wrong! Maybe it wasn't against the Rules, but using knowledge from a later time in an earlier one seemed like major cheating. Like gambling on the stock market with inside information.

"The story came out in September 1917." Malcolm looked at me.

My stomach sank. That's what happened to the German spy's documents? They became fodder for a story? Had Doyle lied to me? "It better be a great story," I said bitterly.

"You don't know that Doyle built the story from your brief-case documents. You have to read it before you judge him. Anyway, you can ask him yourself when you go back to talk about Mom."

"Ask what?" Dad said, coming out of the café.

Malcolm was right, there was no point in speculating about the documents. Better to change the subject. "I was just asking Malcolm if he knew where Doyle got the idea for Sherlock Holmes."

Malcolm didn't miss a beat. "The real life inspiration was a doctor that Doyle studied with in Edinburgh when he was a medical student. Dr. Joseph Bell. He showed his classes how to use close observation to make a diagnosis. To demonstrate, he would often pick a stranger and deduce his occupation and recent activities, just through careful, detailed observation. He used these same skills with dead bodies, figuring out time and cause of death by noticing small details. Basically, he was like a medical, forensic detective before those sciences existed, and he was even called upon by Scotland police to help solve crimes."

"So there was a real Sherlock Holmes?" I wondered if Doyle made up anything, or if he just borrowed from people he knew, the way he'd taken my spy documents for his story's plot. Maybe he wasn't as smart or as creative as I'd thought. Which meant maybe he could be completely wrong about Mom, about time travel, about everything.

"You sound disappointed," Dad noted. "Just because you

base a character on a real person, that doesn't mean you're less of a writer. A lot of authors draw on their own personal experiences. It's what they do with those kernels of truth, how they turn them into compelling fiction, that makes them great writers."

"I guess," I said, though I wasn't at all sure I agreed. It was kind of like the old argument about drawing versus photography. If I drew a pencil so well that it looked real, that was an artistic achievement. If I took a photo of it, that was boring and ordinary. There had to be some effort involved, more than pushing a button – the creative work of making something out of nothing.

"Tell you what," Dad suggested. "Let's head to 221B Baker Street. I know Arthur Conan Doyle didn't really live there, but Sherlock Holmes did and there's a Holmes museum there now. Seems like a good place to find the Touchstone you need to get you back to Doyle." Dad leaned over the map he'd spread out on the table. "Here." He pointed. "That's where the house is, not too far from here."

Not far, I noticed, from Doyle's real home, either. That would save me some walking.

We had money, there were buses and the tube, but we decided to walk, in case we passed a possible Touchstone on the way. It was strange to walk back along some of the same streets I'd taken last century. Then it had been bleak winter. Now it was bright summer. And instead of rooftops lined with chimneys belching sooty smoke, there was a hot blue July sky over roofs punctuated with satellite dishes. But the biggest difference was the smell – hot tar, car exhaust, and wafts of garbage, but nothing like the oppressive stench of a century ago.

As we got close, I could feel it, the vibrations of a Touch-stone. I scanned the street, searching for a fountain, a sculpture, a clock tower, anything that had to do with time. When I saw it, I laughed. The perfect Touchstone, one that was almost a joke.

"What's so funny?" Malcolm asked.

"The Touchstone. Can't you see it?"

Malcolm scanned ahead of us. There, to the right, was the quaint awning declaring the Sherlock Holmes Museum. On the corner of the block was the square address label for Baker Street.

"You mean?"

"Elementary, my dear Malcolm, elementary!" I put on my best British accent, which was admittedly not very good.

"The statue?" Dad pointed. "Of course!"

There it stood, across from 221B Baker street, one of the

most famous addresses in history – a larger-than-life-sized statue of Sherlock Holmes, complete with cloak, deerstalker hat, and pipe.

"Are you ready, Mira? Do you know what you're going to do?" Dad took my hand. "Do you want to do this?"

"Yes, Dad. You said you had faith in me, re-member? You need to give up control, just like

Mom does. You have to trust me to take care of myself."

Dad smiled. "You're absolutely right. I do." He stepped back and put his arm around Malcolm. They watched as I concentrated on Doyle, on how he'd looked the last time I'd seen him, on the briefcase between us, as I reached out my hand and grazed my fingers on the statue's cape. Electricity crackled from the bronze into me, charging the air, as suns swirled around me, moons rose and set, smoke billowed and shadows flitted before me – horses, carriages, carts, trucks, cars, buses, lorries, the life of the street splintering and coming together like images on a kaleidoscope. I felt dizzy and queasy until suddenly the ground stopped shuddering.

It was freezing cold, the air heavy with soot, so I knew even before I looked around that I was back in the past, sometime that smelled exactly like the winter of 1917. Maybe I was finally learning to control my gift after all. I examined my clothing – yep, the same dress I'd worn before. Not any cleaner, either. I wondered if there was a time travel costume closet. Where did the clothes come from anyway, or were these my jeans and T-shirt transformed? Something to ask Morton or Mom about in the future. I mean, when I next had the chance.

I was still on Baker Street with the exact same buildings, but no Sherlock Holmes statue or museum, though a strange figure was knocking on the door of 221B. Was somebody actually expecting to find the great detective at home? Who really lived there and how much did they get pestered by fans of the fictional detective?

I watched, hoping to catch a glimpse of whoever opened the door. Only the door didn't open. The knocker rapped louder. Still no answer. Disappointed, the person turned to walk away. As they got closer, I recognized the beautiful face beneath the dove-gray hat.

It was the Watcher. Again.

I shivered, partly from the dank chill, partly from icy dread. I pushed flat against the wall of an alley, holding my breath against the rancid stench. How could she bounce back and forth in time so perfectly, almost as if she were tracking me? And if she  could follow me that way, why couldn't she find Mom? Long, slow minutes ticked by as the Watcher disappeared, heading toward the green swath of Regent's Park. She hadn't seen me! She hadn't even sensed me. So was her being here just a coincidence? I didn't know what to think, except that I had to be careful, extra alert.

It was getting too dark and cold for the long walk to Doyle's apartment. I glanced around for a pub, a shop, somewhere I could get warm, but because of the blackout shades, I couldn't see any lights. There wasn't anywhere obvious to go, except the place right in front of me, where the Watcher had tried to get in. If she wasn't looking for me, what did she want here? I wondered as I knocked on the door at 221B Baker Street.

Nobody had responded when the Watcher had pounded on the door, but this time the black-lacquered door opened.

I'd half-hoped Mom would be there, or Doyle, or maybe Morton, ready to show me where to go next. I'd expected a maid or a butler, one of the vast class of servants that existed in London, like a city within the city.

The person who stood there wasn't any of these.

A jolt of recognition hit me. The light, curly hair, the wide gray eyes, the broad shoulders and slim build. It was Clark, who I'd last seen in front of Mrs. Pankhurst's house. Suddenly I felt hot, despite the winter cold. And embarrassed.

We both stood there gawking. He seemed as surprised to see me as I was to see him.

"Miriam Lodge, as I live and breathe," he said. He didn't sound angry. In fact, he seemed pleased and that gave me the courage to smile at him.

"Clark Warden." My voice wobbled and I cleared my throat, steadying myself. "I'm sorry about the last time we saw each other. I really didn't have the time then."

"Of course." The tips of his ears turned pink. Did that mean he still l liked me? "I hope you'll forgive my impertinence."

"There's nothing to forgive. I was delighted by your invitation. I was just busy." All of which was true, especially the delighted part. "Do you work here? This isn't the address you gave for your home."

"Actually, I was waiting for somebody. It's all very mysterious, it is."

I waited for him to explain the mystery, but he stood there, actually scratching his head, as if he could scritch his mind into making sense of whatever the problem was.

"Um, can I come in? You can explain it all to me," I suggested. I was too curious now to look for Doyle. It was such an odd coincidence that Clark of all people was here. In this place of powerful mysteries – Sherlock Holmes' fabled home. The whole thing smelled significant, full of meaning, the way a Touchstone did. Plus, I'll admit it, I was happy to see him and would a short visit with him really make a difference in dealing with Mom? If I couldn't have a boyfriend, at least I could have some friendly minutes with a boy I liked.

"Of course, of course," stammered Clark, still looking dazed. And encouragingly flustered. I took his embarrassment as a good sign. "There's a front parlor we can use." Right off the entryway, a door led to a small waiting room. Some fussy chairs, end tables with lace doilies, a low table between them with, of course, a teapot and cups. It felt like a little old lady's home. It kind of smelled like one – a mix of mothballs and wet cat.

"So why are you here? What's the mystery?" I asked. Maybe Clark would help me figure all this out. Maybe he was meant to be more than a passing acquaintance.

"Please keep your voice down," Clark whispered, sitting down close to me. "I don't want to disturb the household. This room is for visitors, for the tourists who show up looking for Mr. Holmes. The woman who lives here gave up trying to explain he's not a real person. Now she just sets them in this room to wait for his return."

"But he'll never come!" I whispered back.

"Precisely! They sit and sit until they give up and go away. But leastways, they don't bother the household no more."

"Don't tell me you're waiting for Holmes yourself." It felt like we were the only two people awake in London, all alone in the quiet house. It was strangely intimate. Like a date, almost.

"Of course not! I know he's just a character in a book. Not even a very realistic one, if you ask me. All that careful observation guff! It's a trick, I tell you, like the shell game barkers play at the fair, having you guess which cup has a pea under it when the pea is in the palm of their hand the whole time."

"I don't know about realistic, but they're fun stories to read, even if I never can solve the mystery."

"Of course you can't! You don't know that the incriminating footprint is from a shoe sold only in New Zealand. Nor that the ashes left behind were from a distinctive cigarette made in a small village in Spain. Which means Mr. X must be the culprit because there he is – wearing those shoes and smoking that cigarette!"

"That's a bit of an exaggeration."

"Is it? Is it really?" Clark waggled his eyebrows to show me how preposterous it all was. Neither of us was in a hurry to get to the point. Why Clark was here, what the mystery was. It was just so easy to talk.

Best of all, Clark clearly wasn't mad at me. He liked me, "liked" liked me. Which I shouldn't care about. But still. "Forget about all that," I said, finally getting serious. "Why are you here?"

"A lady sent me."

"Which lady? And why here?" It was all getting curiouser and curiouser, as another British writer would say. I wondered suddenly if Lewis Carroll, who wrote *Alice in Wonderland,* had been at that publishing reception. I wasn't sure exactly when he lived, but late nineteenth-century, early twentieth sounded right. Where was Malcolm when I needed him!

"She didn't say her name, or if she did, I forgot it. But she was dressed like a person of quality, so I didn't pry. She came to my father's  shop and said she'd pay me good money to come to this house tonight. She told me about this room being free, all I had to do was say I was waiting for Holmes. Which I did."

"But why? Are you spying on somebody?" I had a sneaking suspicion I knew who the lady was. And that she would use Clark this way seemed mean.

"No, not at all." Clark reached into his pocket and took out a folded piece of paper. "I'm delivering a message."

I didn't say anything. Now I knew who the lady was.

"To you." Clark handed me the paper. "Odd coincidence, isn't it? She didn't say it'd be you – just that I should open the door to the second person who knocked and give them this. Not the first, definitely not the first, but the second. She was very insistent on that."

I took the paper with numb fingers. So Mom knew the Watcher would come here, she knew I would. And she knew about Clark. How? Had she seen it in a time travel visit? Just giving a note to me in this convoluted way was a message in itself.

"I'm glad to see you again. Of course I am. But I'm surprised it happened this way." Clark looked at me with hopeful eyes. "I was still thinking maybe you'd come to see me."

"I really meant to, but I've been busy." I felt miserable lying to him again, but what choice did I have? All the good feelings from the previous five minutes were wiped away. Mom was telling me I couldn't be friends with Clark. Not now, not ever.

I stared at the message, afraid to open it.

"Do you want me to stay with you for awhile? Or walk you home? You weren't expecting to find Holmes when you knocked, were you?" Clark was being so sweet. What would he think if he knew the truth?

"No, no, I'm fine by myself." I hated the idea of disappointing him – and myself – yet again. But that's all I could ever be to him – a big disappointment. I touched his arm lightly, wishing I could do more. "I appreciate the offer. And if things were different. . ." I trailed off. He could imagine what he wanted, that I had a sweetheart, was running away from a cruel husband, had signed up to be a nurse on the front, anything to explain my distance.

The note felt heavy in my hands. I needed Clark to go away, to leave me alone to figure this out. "You go on, then," I urged. "I'll come see you tomorrow, if I can." But I wouldn't. I hoped to be back with Dad and Malcolm – and Mom.

"All right, then." Clark smiled and stretched out his hand. I got up to shake it, wishing we could be more than friends, knowing we couldn't. His hand felt warm and rough in mine. I let go, the door swung open, and he was gone.

Once the front door had closed, I unfolded the paper. It was in Mom's handwriting.

Mira,

You must believe me – I know what I'm doing. The fact you have this note is proof of that. I know you've talked to Doyle and that you'll be at 221B Baker Street tonight. You think you understand some things better, but you're looking through a glass darkly, at warped images only half-understood. This letter is meant to clear your vision.

You know now that it is very rare for a mother and daughter to both be time travelers. It's a very strong bond, since in essence, we're a different iteration of the same flow of time. We already temporally influence each other, your existence a direct result of mine. It's why I'm so careful not to see you in the past, and it's also why, despite Doyle's arguments, I can help you change your future. I can make a difference for you, though yes, you need to make the actual changes. I'm locating the places on the space-time continuum where it's possible for the lines to diverge safely, like the binary trees Bruno explained to you.

This is one of those times. So believe me when I say you must get the documents to Room 40 now. Trust me, I know what I'm doing.

Love, Mom

This was the longest, most honest note she'd sent me and I read over and over the part about us both being time travelers, the special connection that gave us. She acted like her getting the note to me was proof of how well she could control things, but she didn't know I'd given the documents away. So maybe she had proved just the opposite.

And anyway, even if I believed her, if we could change my future this way, it was a completely selfish thing to do. And it wasn't worth preventing my Horrible Thing if the unpredictable side effects caused others pain. Either way, I was determined to control my own future, not just do Mom's bidding.

The room was stuffy and warm and my head felt heavy, like it was made of sand. The clock on the mantle read just a little past nine. It wasn't that late, but who knew what time it was for my body? The middle of the night, my drooping eyelids said. I snuggled into the chair, the note safe and warm in my pocket, and closed my eyes, just for a second.

Only of course, it was more than a second. When I woke up, light was streaming through the narrow gap in the curtains and I could hear the clopping of hooves, the rumble of motors from the street outside. I stretched my stiff muscles and ran my fingers through the tangles of my hair, trying not to look like someone who'd spent the night at a bus station.

I meant to creep out of the house quietly, but before I could get to the front door, an older woman swept in, her chest like the prow of a boat. A lace cap with ribbons was pinned to the back of her hair, and glasses slid down to the tip of her nose. She looked exactly the way I'd imagined the owner of all the fussy frou-frou ornaments in the parlor.

"My dear!" she bellowed. "Have you spent the night waiting for Sherlock Holmes? As you can see, he won't be back anytime soon. Out in the country, visiting his good friend Dr. Watson." She sounded like a goose with a chest cold, her voice deep and nasal.

"Oh, of course," I mumbled. "Please excuse me. I didn't mean to fall asleep. The room is so cozy, you see." I gestured to indicate how all the doilies evoked warmth and comfort. As if.

"You aren't the first, and I dare say, you won't be the last, to have a wee nap in the parlor." The woman chuckled. I wondered how many Holmes fans camped out here. I supposed I was lucky to have the place to myself.

"Well, I'll be off now." I pulled my cloak around my shoulders, feeling oddly like I should give her a tip or something. Instead I gave a limp wave and opened the door, relieved to get away.

The morning air was already tinged with fireplace smoke, car exhaust, burning coal, rotting vegetables, and a hint of baking bread. It was early, but the streets were crowded, a buzz of energy surging through the groups of people as they headed to work. Something had happened, I could feel it. I searched for a news vendor on my way to Doyle's and was stopped by a headline blaring from the stand:

WILL WILSON WAGE WAR?

I found the date first, March 4, 1917, then quickly scanned the story. The very first paragraph mentioned the Zimmermann Telegram. It was followed by a copy of the entire message:

FROM 2ND FROM LONDON # 5747.

WE INTEND TO BEGIN ON THE FIRST OF FEBRUARY UN-
RESTRICTED SUBMARINE WARFARE. WE SHALL ENDEAVOR IN
SPITE OF THIS TO KEEP THE UNITED STATES OF AMERI-
CA NEUTRAL. IN THE EVENT OF THIS NOT SUCCEEDING, WE
MAKE MEXICO A PROPOSAL OF ALLIANCE ON THE FOLLOWING
BASIS: MAKE WAR TOGETHER, MAKE PEACE TOGETHER, GEN-
EROUS FINANCIAL SUPPORT AND AN UNDERSTANDING ON OUR
PART THAT MEXICO IS TO RECONQUER THE LOST TERRITORY
IN TEXAS, NEW MEXICO, AND ARIZONA. THE SETTLEMENT IN
DETAIL IS LEFT TO YOU. YOU WILL INFORM THE PRESIDENT
OF THE ABOVE MOST SECRETLY AS SOON AS THE OUTBREAK OF
WAR WITH THE UNITED STATES OF AMERICA IS CERTAIN AND
ADD THE SUGGESTION THAT HE SHOULD, ON HIS OWN INITIA-
TIVE, INVITE JAPAN TO IMMEDIATE ADHERENCE AND AT THE
SAME TIME MEDIATE BETWEEN JAPAN AND OURSELVES. PLEASE
CALL THE PRESIDENT'S ATTENTION TO THE FACT THAT THE
RUTHLESS EMPLOYMENT OF OUR SUBMARINES NOW OFFERS THE
PROSPECT OF COMPELLING ENGLAND IN A FEW MONTHS TO MAKE
PEACE. SIGNED, ZIMMERMANN

I knew the general nature of
the telegram, but I was outraged all
over again, reading the bald offer to
Mexico's president to take control of

the "lost territory" of Texas, New Mexico, and Arizona, as if Germany was standing over the United States, prepared to carve up the country as it pleased.

The article went on to say that the American government was wary that the telegram could be a fake, planted by the British to goad the U.S. into entering the war. They were suspicious despite the contents of a briefcase the Secret Service had obtained that contained incriminating papers documenting German undercover activity on United States soil. And still that hadn't been enough for Wilson. The last straw, according to the reporter, happened the previous day at a press conference, when Zimmermann himself told an American journalist, "I cannot deny it. It is true."

England now waited, as did the rest of the world. What would President Wilson do?

I read the article a second time, slowly, to make sure I hadn't missed anything. A briefcase with incriminating papers – that had to be the one I'd stolen. So Doyle had passed it on, as Mom wanted. And that hadn't changed anything, just as he had predicted. The Secret Service had those papers for over a month. But Malcolm had said that the Zimmerman Telegram was what pushed Wilson into finally declaring war on Germany. Here it was, six weeks after the president had seen the devious plan, along with records of payments to German saboteurs, and nothing had changed.

A sour taste rose in my mouth. What if Mom and I had ruined things, not made them better? What if the briefcase documents, instead of pushing Wilson to believe the telegram was real, had convinced him that there was a whole industry of forged papers being fed to him by the British? Maybe it was too much, too convenient, for him to rely on them?

But Zimmermann himself admitted he sent the telegram! What more could it possibly take? I hated to think that I'd helped the ugly plot along, that because of me, Mexico would invade the United States, Germany would win the war, and the shape of the world would be changed forever. When I went back to the present, what would I find? Would England be a German territory? Would everyone be speaking German and eating wurst?

I tore myself away from the newspaper. Now I recognized the energy I felt in the street. It was hope, hope that America would finally enter the war. But I didn't feel hopeful at all. If Wilson was going to declare war, wouldn't that have already happened? What else could he possibly be waiting for? Why didn't Congress do something?

If only Doyle had some answers! Maybe his clear thinking would save the day, just as it always did in the Sherlock Holmes stories. I pounded on his front door, impatient in my fear. "Please be home, please, please, please," I chanted under my breath.

The jowly butler opened the door, clearly offended by my mussed-up appearance. Before he could slam the door in my face, I reminded him I'd been there before, that I was a friend of Doyle, and explained that I'd had an unfortunate accident, hence my less-than-fresh look this fine morning, could I please see the master now, it was extremely urgent. The words rushed out before the gloved hand could push me away. There was a moment of awkward silence. Then a curt "I see, miss" from the butler. I sighed in relief as he opened the door wider and gestured for me to come in, though he looked suspiciously at my shoes as if I was about to track in dog poop.

While Marston went to inform the master that I was there, I paced along the bookshelves in the study nervously, picking up things and putting them down, while the panic rose higher inside of me. What had I done? Why had I ever listened to Mom? Anger mixed with the dread – I was furious at Mom, angrier than I'd ever been, even that time when she'd thrown away all my sketchbooks in a fit of manic cleaning. I thought of what Sylvia had said about the fight with her mother, how she was hurt more deeply because she'd been struck, not by an enemy, but by someone close to her.

The door creaked open, interrupting my miserable stewing. Doyle walked in and I immediately felt calmer.

"Good morning, Miss Lodge. I didn't expect you!" He looked surprised, but not annoyed, which I took as a good sign. "Please have a seat. Marston is bringing tea and crumpets. You look like you could do with some."

I perched on the edge of a chair, too jittery to relax. "Did we ruin everything? Did we make things worse?"

"Worse? How? You seem quite upset. Has something happened?" Doyle settled into the big leather chair as if all was right with the world.

"I saw the newspaper! Wilson still hasn't declared war on Germany. You said you'd give the War Office the briefcase, but that hasn't shortened the war – it may have prolonged it, convinced Wilson that everything was fake, all propaganda planted by your government. Or maybe you didn't give the briefcase to anyone at all. I know about your story, the one about Holmes catching the Nazi spy. Did you use the documents for a story?"

"First of all, let me reassure you, *His Last Bow* may have indeed have been inspired by those papers, but I did not reveal any military secrets. Besides, that's what writers do. We take bits from our lives and transform them into fiction. In this case, the documents simply suggested the activities of German spies here in England, not a preposterous thing to imagine even without having seen the briefcase. Ah, here's Marston with the tea!" Doyle leaned

forward and poured out two cups.

"Secondly, I delivered the briefcase to the War Office, as I said I would. What happened after that, I couldn't say. And finally, your president hasn't declared war yet, but he still may, and my guess is he will." He was exasperatingly calm and fresh, like someone who'd had a good night's sleep.

"Wouldn't he have done that by now? The Zimmermann Telegram was supposed to convince him, my brother told me so! But it hasn't! Nothing has!" I blinked away tears of frustration.

"Now, now there! You're quite overreacting. Drink your tea. It will set you right." Doyle hovered over me with a steaming cup.

"Thank you," I sniffled, sipping the hot tea. It seemed silly, but the warmth calmed me. No wonder the British always had tea handy.

"I came because I thought you could convince my mother to come home with me since she won't listen to me. She knew I'd come back, she knew exactly where and when." I explained the whole scenario – Clark hired to wait for me – and showed Doyle the note. "So you can see she was determined to change the past and now she's gone and done it, only she's changed it in the wrong way."

Doyle set his cup down firmly in its saucer with a brittle clink. "You don't know that. I mean to say, yes, you know she's stubborn. But you don't know that she's actually changed anything. The best thing would be for you to go to your present, then you'll know for sure, no more guessing."

"But what if England is run by Nazis when I go back?" My hands shook nervously holding the fragile tea cup.

"Nazis! I hardly think so!" His tone was assured, but how

could he know? "Or you can time travel ahead just a month or so, and you'll see that your president has indeed declared war in his own sweet time."

"Do you know that or you're guessing?" I pressed.

"I know precisely as much as you do, but I'm not leaping to wild conclusions. Terribly un-Holmes-like." He helped himself to a crumpet smeared with jam, as if this kind of conversation were an everyday occurrence. And maybe with him, it was.

It was somehow reassuring to treat this catastrophe like a mystery. I could see the appeal of cold, hard data.

"Here's what we know," Doyle began after swallowing a mouthful of crumpet. "Your mother gave you instructions through Morton to grab the German spy's briefcase and get it to Room 40. You surmised this was to corroborate the Zimmermann Telegram and hasten the United States's entry into the war. But you don't know that was your mother's intent."

I gasped. He was right – I'd assumed that. Malcolm and Dad had too. But what if Mom really wanted to keep America out of the war altogether? How could she possibly dare?

"You, however, passed the briefcase and its contents on to me, which was not your mother's plan. I gave the documents to the War Office, also not your mother's intention. We cannot know the effect of those papers on either this government or yours. But we do know that President Wilson has received ample evidence of Germany's treacherous plots from your Secret Service as well as our government. And we know that Zimmermann himself has admitted the telegram is real."

"Which means I didn't help Mom?" That was a good thing, right?

"If you did, it was an unintentional." Doyle leaned back and smiled confidently, patting his lips with a napkin. "This is what I meant by how impossible it is to control the future by meddling with the past. You can't know with any certainty the consequences of your actions. If only your mother were as sensible as you!"

"She would say she's way more logical, which makes her right, no matter what."

"Well, she isn't right now, despite her supposedly impeccable reasoning skills."

If only I could be as certain as Doyle! I thought he was right. But absolute certainty? No, that eluded me. Another reason he would be more convincing with Mom than me. "I was hoping that since you argue so well, so logically, you could talk to her. Convince her to come back to her right time and leave my future for me to handle. If it isn't too late, that is."

'You're a time traveler." Doyle chuckled. "It's never too late. Time isn't the issue here."

"Then what is?" I asked, draining the last of my tea.

"It's a question of personal responsibility and of family connection. I'm sorry to disappoint you, but I can't convince your mother."

"Can't or won't?" I asked.

"Both or either." Doyle was beginning to sound like an *Alice in Wonderland* character, making no sense at all. "I mean," he clarified, "only you can do that. There isn't enough logic in the world to sway her. This argument can only be won with emotion, by her listening to her daughter with her heart, not her head. As rational as she is, that's really the only way to convince her. She needs to learn to trust you."

My own heart sank. That was a losing proposition.

Doyle paused, then leaned forward urgently. "I don't know you well, Mira, but you're clearly a strong, stubborn young lady. You're smart and resourceful. You'll find a way, I'm sure of it. Just remember, your future belongs to you, only to you. That's what your mother needs to know."

"So you won't help me." I felt like a deflated balloon.

"I would if I could, truly. But some tasks are yours alone. I'm wise enough to recognize that even if your mother isn't. More tea?" Doyle held the pot over my empty cup.

I nodded, miserable. "And what happens with the war?"

"We'll find out, won't we? The future awaits." Doyle didn't seem at all worried. In fact, he sounded encouraging. "Now would you like a crumpet before you go?"

That was a gentle way of pushing me out the door. I'd do what he suggested, look for a Touchstone, find Dad and Malcolm, and see what had changed. Malcolm! That reminded me – I took out my sketchbook, opened it to a blank page and handed it to Doyle.

"If you don't mind, please, my brother is a huge fan and would love your autograph."

"You know the Rules," Doyle said.

"But I'm not bringing back anything from the past. My notebook is from the present and it always manages to travel with me."

"I suppose that's all right, then," Doyle decided, signing with a flourish.

"Thank you," I said. "For everything." As I turned to go, I noticed an odd photograph of a girl with paper doll fairies fluttering in front of her. It seemed out of place there, next to a telescope and a compass. "Is that your daughter?" I asked. "She likes to play with fairies?" I expected him to scoff at her imaginary friends. But he didn't.

"That's not my daughter and those are real fairies, not idle toys."

"Real fairies?" Was he teasing me?

"Can't you see that image is proof of the existence of these incredible creatures?" Doyle sounded serious. "Surely if you believe in time travel, you can believe what's right in front of your eyes."

"But those are obviously just paper cutouts, nothing that's really alive!" My stomach dropped. Was Doyle pulling my leg or did he really believe this nonsense? He didn't look like he was joking. Just the opposite. Which meant he wasn't really the king of logical thinking. Had he been telling me the truth about time travel? Was Mom right after all?

No, even if Doyle was wrong, Mom was still being selfish.

Scratch that, Doyle was definitely wrong about the fairies. Mom was wrong about changing things for me. They were both wrong!

Doyle looked ready for an argument, but I'd had enough. "Well, anyway, good luck," I said, shaking Doyle's hand one last time. I'd learned a lot from him, no matter what. Mostly, to trust myself.

I paused at the corner, trying to figure out what my gut told me to do. I didn't believe in fairies, that was for sure, and I hoped I hadn't made an enormous mistake with the briefcase. But Doyle was right about one thing – I was the only one who could see my future clearly, who could make the right choices for myself. And right now, I wanted to go back to my right time, where I belonged.

I remembered that the British Museum was near Doyle's house, full of Touchstones. Those, at least, were real. From a block away, I could feel the force radiating from an Egyptian sphinx, posted outside the main entry. I didn't even need to go inside. As I drew closer, the pull was so strong, it made me dizzy. I wobbled closer and closer, picturing Dad and Malcolm, red double-decker buses, a hot sunny day in modern London. Then I reached out and touched the tawny paw.

Purple lights swirled, snow fell and melted, fog rolled in and out, blazing hot days sizzled into freezing nights until the ground stilled underneath me, and I caught my breath, steady and clearheaded again.

July 9

I was still in front of the British Museum, but now a wrought iron fence ringed the building, and big buses lumbered past, dropping off hordes of tourists. I was back in my jeans and sneakers, my sketchbook still safely tucked in my pocket. But where were Dad and Malcolm? I wasn't sure whether to head for the hotel or back to Baker Street.

The sun was high overhead, so not many hours had passed since seeing them in the café

— if this was still the same day. I guessed they'd be close to the Sherlock Holmes museum. Maybe they'd even gone in while waiting for me. I hurried along the same streets I'd walked a hundred years earlier. Strange how much had changed and how much was

exactly the same. The same! So England hadn't become a German territory! There were no giant Nazi banners, like I'd imagined, and all the signs were in English. In fact, everything looked the way it had when we'd first arrived from Rome.

I felt light and airy with relief. Mom hadn't changed things after all, that much Doyle was right about. So Wilson must have entered the war, and the briefcase of documents had made no difference. Phew! It was funny, well not ha-ha funny, but funny-ironic, that before, in Paris and Rome, I'd been trying so hard to make the changes Mom wanted. In fact, I'd felt like I'd failed her horribly. Now it was the opposite. I desperately wanted to be sure nothing was altered, and it was Mom who was disappointing me.

As I rounded the corner of Baker Street, I was blinded by the glare from the Sherlock Holmes statue, shrouded by strange yellow-purple lights. Then the lights vanished and I could see Dad and Malcolm, both staring at the sculpture.

"Dad! Malcolm!" I yelled, waving my arms.

"Mira?" Dad turned around, startled.

"What were those lights? Some kind of modern art exhibit?" I asked.

"Those lights were you! You just touched the statue and

vanished in these weird, pulsing colors!" Malcolm goggled at me.

"You mean I got here in time to see myself time travel?" Now my head was really spinning.

"Well, right afterwards. You didn't see yourself, did you? Just the lights, right?" Dad pulled me in for a hug, as if checking to see I was really in front of him.

"I'm okay, really. I always see lights like that when I touch a Touchstone. But from the inside. It's different seeing them from the outside."

"Different how?" Malcolm asked.

"It's more normal from here." I explained the way images flashed around me, sometimes the history of the object through the centuries, sometimes the days moving quickly through the cycles of sunrise, sunset, through the seasons. Everything a blur of motion, light, and darkness.

"That is so cool! And look at how good you're getting at this! I don't know how many days passed for you in World War I London, but you weren't gone more than the blink of an eye here." Malcolm nodded approvingly.

"So what happened? Did you see Mom?" Dad always asked the same thing. With the worry notched up each time.

"First you need to tell me that Wilson declared war on Germany. And tell me the date."

"What? Why?" Malcolm took out his phone and started swiping the screen, right into research mode.

"I'll explain it all later. But I've got to know that first!"

"Let's go to a café then. There's no Wi-Fi here. But can't you talk while we walk?" Malcolm held the phone out like a dowser searching for water, checking to see if Wi-Fi would suddenly pop up. After being in a time of horse and buggies, it was odd to see technology again and how reliant on it we were. It seemed a passing phase, just like the steam-driven trucks were on the streets of World War I London.

I described the newspaper, Mom's note, her whole set-up while Dad led us down the street to a café he remembered passing with a Wi-Fi sign in the window. By the time we'd settled down at a table, Malcolm was already looking for answers.

"It's okay, Mira. I don't see anything different from what I learned in class. Arthur Zimmermann admitted sending the wire at a press conference on March 3, 1917, just like you said."

"But what happened after the press conference?" I was halfway reassured, but needed to know that Wilson had entered war the way he was supposed to.

"There was another speech, this one on March 29, a few weeks later." Malcolm kept on reading. "Zimmermann stated again that the telegram was genuine, explaining that, of course, Germany would only put such a plan in action if the United States entered the war. And that threat finally tipped the balance. Wilson declared war on April 4, 1917."

"Thank goodness!" I let out a long breath. "Mom could have ruined everything, she's so obsessed with saving me!" I told them about my visit with Doyle, how he wasn't so trustworthy after all. I mean, really, a grown man believing in fairies! And I filled in the parts of the story I hadn't told them before, about getting arrested, about the Watcher's threats. "The one thing I'm sure of now in all of this is that we've got to make Mom stop."

Dad looked stunned. "You were arrested again? You could have been in prison? Whether Mom's right or wrong doesn't matter anymore – you can't take these risks!"

"But I have to. Until I get Mom home, there's no other choice."

Dad looked ready to cry. "What if I lose both of you?"

"That's won't happen. You have to trust me, just like Mom needs to." I rubbed my sore knee under the table, hoping the ache would go away. If Dad saw me limping, it would really put him over the edge.

"Mira's right," Malcolm said. "And look how much better she is at time travel now. Mom needs to see how capable Mira is. Isn't that every parent's job, to know when to let go? Mira's the only one who can show her that."

I felt a rush of gratitude for his support. "It's not about Mom saving me anymore. It's about me saving Mom – from the

Watcher and from herself."

"There's nothing for you to do right now," Dad insisted. "No more time travel until Mom sends us another postcard, okay? And promise me that the next time you go into the past, it will only be to help her come home. That's it, nothing else. No more messing with history. We've got to stand together as a family, that's the only way to convince Mom."

I nodded. "I wish you could come back in time with me – that might shock her into listening. That reminds me, I have something for you, since you're stuck in the present." I took out my sketchbook, opened it to the right page, and handed it to Malcolm.

"You're kidding! Sir Arthur Conan Doyle," he read. "Even if he wasn't as much like Sherlock Holmes as we wish." He leafed through the pages. "Did you draw him somewhere in here? H. G. Wells? Beatrix Potter?"

"Yes, I sketched them all. Not very well, but I'll show you." I took back the notebook and was flipping through the pages when I noticed something that didn't belong there. On the page facing my clumsy squirrel sketch was something I hadn't drawn at all – a cat hunched over a saucer of milk.

Written below it was the inscription "From one artist to another, yours in pencil, Beatrix Potter."

"Look!" I said, wobbly with wonder. "Beatrix Potter drew in my notebook! And she said I'm an artist!"

"You are!" Malcolm said. "A really good one!"

Dad grinned, pink with pride. He believed in me – I could see it in his face.

"I wish I could show Mom," I said.

"You will, I'm sure of it." Dad nodded. "You're going to show Mom a lot of things, just like you've shown me."

The waiter interrupted us, handing out menus. The drawing on the front featured a sphinx for some reason. I smiled, thinking of all the Touchstones in the British Museum.

And suddenly I knew what we had to do. No more waiting for postcards, no more following Mom through time. Instead, we would figure out where (when?) she was and I would go there and bring her back. We just had to figure out how. The surge of energy I'd felt in the British Museum each time I pulled back from a Touchstone would help me somehow. I was sure of it.

"You're right!" I said to Dad. "We're all going to show Mom. It's our turn to lead the way."

Malcolm grinned at me. "Are you thinking what I think you're thinking?"

"We agreed, no more time travel until we heard from Mom," Dad repeated, looking around the café nervously as if one of Mom's postcards was on its way this very second.

"I never said that," I corrected him. "I agreed not to try to change history. The only thing we need to change is Mom's mind."

"We don't know what she's trying to change, so how can we possibly guess where she is, when she is? She seems to pick completely random times and places." Dad threw up his hands.

"I have to trust my instincts more," I said. "I think I can find her."

Malcolm grinned at me. "I know you can. And I'm going to find that Watcher. If we follow her, she might lead us to Mom."

"How are you going to track her? I thought she was tracing me somehow. . . or all of us."

"I don't know yet, but seeing her here in our time makes me think it's possible. Besides, that's something I can do while you search in the past."

So no more waiting for postcards. Malcolm had his job and I had mine. It was time for me to time travel on my own. I leaned back in the chair, looking out into the traffic on the London streets. The cars and buses swirled by, circling a tall column with a statue perched on top of it. Hmm, I wondered. Could that be a Touchstone? When did I want to go this time?

Malcolm followed my gaze. "Not London," he said. "It has to somewhere else. Mom always changes countries."

"You're probably right," I admitted. I let my eyes glaze over until the cars were streaks of color moving by, the same way lights and images flashed around me whenever I reached out to a Touchstone. I felt time flow around me, like currents of wind, and I knew,

I just knew, where we had to go.

I turned to Dad, smiling. "Are you ready for another Wonder? Another city?"

"Are we really doing this, Mira?" That was Dad's way of agreeing.

Yes, yes, we really were.

Author's Note

The story of the Zimmermann Telegram is true, as is the Affair of the Purloined Briefcase. Mira, of course, didn't really steal the briefcase, but it was taken from a suspected German spy, Heinrich Albert. This is a case where truth is stranger than fiction because an American Secret Service agent was following Albert, then commercial attaché to the Imperial German Ambassador to the United States, on and off buses in Washington D.C., when Albert conveniently left his briefcase on a tram. The agent grabbed it and found a treasure trove of sensitive documents detailing how Albert had spent twenty-seven million dollars building up a spy network and financing attacks on munitions plants and shipping. One of the German saboteurs, Lothar Witzke, helped plan the July 1916 Black Tom explosion in New Jersey -- the one that pocked the Statue of Liberty with shrapnel – and carried out the March 1917 explosion at Mare Island Navel Shipyard near Vallejo, north of San Francisco. Despite these acts of aggression, along with Germany's blatant plotting with Mexico to stir up a war on the southwest border of the United States, President Wilson was determined to avoid entering the war. It was the Zimmermann Telegram, with its promises to Mexico to regain the territories of Texas, New Mexico, and Arizona, that finally tipped the balance.

Room 40, the code crackers, and specifically Nigel de Grey all really existed.

As described by Mira, the British women's suffrage movement was divided by the war. The militant group founded by Emmeline Pankhurst agreed to ease up pressure on the government in order to support the government and the troops in the fight against Germany. Before the war, Emmeline's group was considered wildly radical, advocating not only for the vote, but also for equal rights in divorce and inheritance. Emmeline didn't shy away from aggressive tactics, saying "Deeds, not words, was to be our permanent motto." The first prison sentence she served hardened her determination. She described her life in jail as "like a human being in the process of being turned into a wild beast." Her most famous speech, "Freedom or Death," was given in Hartford, Connecticut in 1913, a rallying cry for women everywhere to fight for equality. Even while supporting the war effort, Emmeline kept her focus squarely on women's rights.

Sylvia Pankhurst, Emmeline's younger daughter, angrily disagreed with this position, seeing any support of the government as accommodation. She started her own group, the East London Federation of Suffragettes. Protesting not only for the vote, but against the war, Sylvia's group focused on conscientious objectors and the women who worked in factories, doing men's work for women's wages. The two Pankhursts never reconciled, but after the war women were granted the vote on a limited basis. In fact, after World War I, all the Allied countries, beginning with Russia, granted women the right to vote in recognition of their vital contributions during the war. Only France didn't, earning the title of last European country to enfranchise women. Finally in 1944, by a special decree of General de Gaulle, French women were given the right to vote.

In England, women's rights were granted in two stages. In 1918 only women with property and over the age of thirty could vote. Then in 1928, votes were granted to all women over twenty-one.

In the United States, President Wilson punished suffragists much as the British had. Alice Paul, who had met and worked with the Pankhursts in London, insisted on peaceful protests, but she was treated just as harshly as her British counterparts. Paul was imprisoned, force fed, and sent to a sanitarium in an attempt to have her permanently committed as a madwoman. The outraged public reaction saved her, forcing Wilson to support the Nineteenth Amendment, calling for women's suffrage. The House and Senate both passed the measure in 1919, but then three-quarters of the states also had to ratify it. It took a year, but Tennessee became the last vote needed for ratification in August 1920. The session in the state legislature was dramatic, with ratification passing by a single vote – that of Harry Burn, the youngest legislator. He'd planned on voting no, but changed his mind after his mother sent him a telegram, asking him to support women's rights.

Other states followed slowly, though the measure was now part of the Constitution. Maryland finally voted for ratification in 1941, Virginia in 1952, Alabama in 1953, Florida and South Carolina only in 1969. Georgia and Louisiana were very late, ratifying in 1971. Mississippi was the last state, not ratifying until 1984!

Sir Arthur Conan Doyle was famous for creating the brilliantly deductive detective, Sherlock Holmes, but he was also a firm believer in contacting the spirit world. When, in the summer of 1917 (so after the time period of this book, though as Doyle himself says, what's time to a time traveler?), two Yorkshire girls produced "proof" of the existence of fairies using photography, Doyle was one of their staunchest supporters. The pictures of the "Cottingley Fairies" were widely circulated and thousands believed in them, though to our modern eyes, the fairies look like obvious paper cutouts. The two girls admitted their deception only as old women in the early 1980s. Doyle died believing their story to be true. Mira, of course, knew better.

Bibliography

Room 40, British Intelligence:

Andrew, Christopher. *Her Majesty's Secret Service: The Making of the British Intelligence Community*. New York: Viking, 1986.

Beesley, Patrick. *Room 40: British Naval Intelligence, 1914–1918*. Long Acre, London: Hamish Hamilton Ltd, 1982.

Denniston, Robin. *Thirty Secret Years: A.G. Denniston's Work for Signals Intelligence 1914-1944*. Polperro Heritage Press, 2007.

Gannon, Paul. *Inside Room 40: The Codebreakers of World War I*. London: Ian Allen Publishing, 2011.

Hoy, Hugh Cleveland. *40 O.B. or How the War Was Won*. London: Hutchison & Co., 1932.

Johnson, John. *The Evolution of British Sigint, 1653–1939*. London: H.M.S.O.,1997.

Tuchman Barbara, *The Zimmermann Telegram*. New York: Ballantine Books, 1958.

World War I and London:

Bailey, Paul. *The Oxford Book of London*. Oxford: Oxford University Press, 1995.

Carradice, Phil. *The Great War, An Illustrated History*. Stroud: Amberley, 2010.

Castle, Ian. *London 1917-18, The Bomber Blitz*, Oxford: Osprey Publishing, 2010.

de Groot, Gerard. *The First World War,* New York: Palgrave, 2001.

Graysel, Susan R. *Women and the First World War*, London: Pearson Education, 2002.

Heyman, Neil. *Daily Life During World War I*. London: Greenwood Press, 2002.

Hochschild, Adam. *To End All Wars*. New York: Houghton Mifflin

Harcourt, 2011.

Holmes, Burton. *The World 100 Years Ago*. Philadelphia: Chelsea House, 1998.

Hyde, Andrew. *The First Blitz, the German Air Campaign Against Britain 1917-1918*. Barnsley: Lee Cooper, 2002.

Marwick, Arthur. *Women at War*. London: Croom Helm, 1977.

Rowe Jr., Josiah. *Letters From a World War I Aviator*. Boston: Sinclair Press, 1986.

Thom, Deborah. *Nice Girls and Rude Girls: Women Workers in World War I*. New York: I.B. Tauris Publishers, 1998.

Tuchman, Barbara. *The Guns of August*. New York: Ballantine Books edition, 1994.

Tuchman, Barbara. *The Proud Tower*. New York: Ballantine Books edition,1996.

Westwell, Ian. *World War I, Day by Day*. London: Windmill Books Ltd, 2012.

Women's Suffrage:

Eustance, Claire; Ryan, Joan; and Ugolini, Laura, editors. *A Suffrage Reader*. London: Leicester University Press, 2000.

Fell, Alison S. and Sharp, Ingrid, editors. *The Women's Movement in Wartime*. New York: Palgrave, 2007.

Pankhurst, E. Sylvia. *The Life of Emmeline Pankhurst*. London: T. Werner Laurie Ltd, 1935.

Pankhurst, E. Sylvia. *The Suffragette*. New York: Sturgis & Walton Co, 1911.

Pugh, Martin. *The Pankhursts*. London: Penguin Books, 2001.

Smith, Angela. *The Second Battlefield: Women, Modernism and the First World War*. Manchester: Manchester University Press, 2000.

Vellacott, Jo. *Pacifists, Patriots, and the Vote*. New York: Palgrave, 2007.

Sir Arthur Conan Doyle:

Doyle, Arthur Conan. *Memories and Adventures,* Cambridge: Cambridge University Press, 2012.

Lellenberg, Jon; Stashower, Daniel; and Foley, Charles. *Arthur Conan Doyle: A Life in Letters.* New York: Penguin Press, 2007.

Miller, Russell. *The Adventures of Arthur Conan Doyle: A Biography.* New York: Thomas Dunne Books, 2008.

Stashower, Daniel. *Teller of Tales: The Life of Arthur Conan Doyle.* New York: Henry Holt & Co., 1999

Visual Digital Resources:

Wrenn, Eddie. The London Daily Mail Online. Images from history: Rarely seen photographs bring 1800s London back to life. www.dailymail.co.uk/news/article-1204508/Images-history -Rarely-seen-photographs-bring-1800s-London-life.html

The History Channel. History of London. www.history.co.uk/study-topics/history-of-london/

Footage Farm. WWI Aviation; London; Bulgaria; Artillery 220672-06. www.youtube.com/watch?v=RX0ONrB1ylQ

bds2014. WW1 Footage. www.youtube.com/watch?v=7XQ_o-rYl-U

allenw195. Zeppelin Bombs London part 1. www.youtube.com/watch?v=KneO_PR17Ys

Film and Video Archive of the Imperial War Museum. Bombing of London - 1917. www.youtube.com/watch?v=3SW-5AYNaUE

Manic Minutes. Murder by Zeppelin! - London Attacked! www.youtube.com/watch?v=e5eU7VJm9MM

SKYteamST. Zeppelin & Gotha in the great war. www.youtube.com/watch?v=6kaQYGuWs14

Stott, David. Postcards of London 1914. www.youtube.com/watch?v=VuoDOx2jJbM

LondonsScreenArchive. Old London Street Scenes (1903). www.youtube.com/watch?v=DVQiEJW7RWg

Acknowledgements

I couldn't have written this book without the help of my insightful writing group – Diane Fraser, Eleanor Vincent, Emily Polsby, Joanne Rocklin, and Susi Jensen. Other readers with brilliant suggestions were Joan Lester, Asa Stahl, Kristen Carvalho, and Elias Stahl. Thank you all for helping me travel through the centuries.

About the Author

     Marissa Moss has written more than 50 books for children. Her popular *Amelia's Notebook* series has sold millions of copies and been translated into five languages. The author has won many awards, including ALA Notable, Best Books in Booklist, Amelia Bloomer Pick of the List, and the California Book Award. Mira's previous adventure, *Mira's Diary: Home Sweet Rome*, was a finalist for the Northern California Book Reviewers' Award.

Read Mira's Other Adventures

Published by Sourcebooks:

Mira's Diary: Lost in Paris (1)

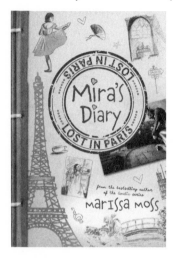

Mira's Diary: Home Sweet Rome (2)

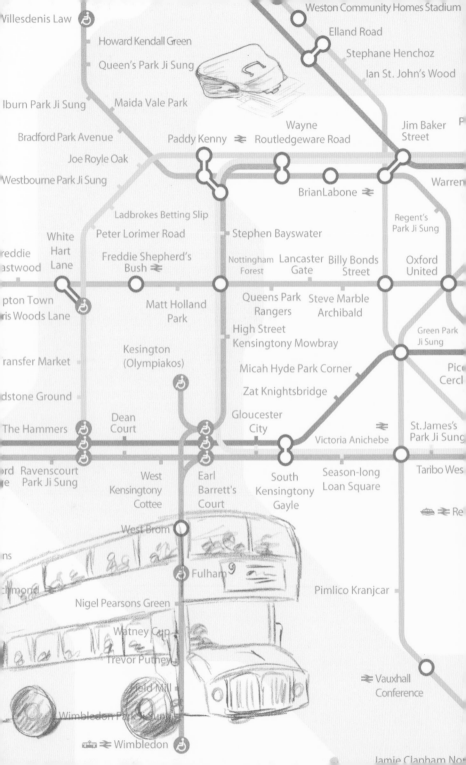

Villesdenis Law

Howard Kendall Green

Queen's Park Ji Sung

Iburn Park Ji Sung

Maida Vale Park

Bradford Park Avenue

Joe Royle Oak

Westbourne Park Ji Sung

Weston Community Homes Stadium

Elland Road

Stephane Henchoz

Ian St. John's Wood

Wayne
Routledgeware Road

Jim Baker
Street

Paddy Kenny

BrianLabone

Warren

Regent's
Park Ji Sung

Ladbrokes Betting Slip

White
Hart
Lane

Peter Lorimer Road

Freddie Shepherd's
Bush

Stephen Bayswater

reddie
astwood

Nottingham   Lancaster   Billy Bonds
Forest   Gate   Street

Oxford
United

pton Town
ris Woods Lane

Matt Holland
Park

Queens Park   Steve Marble
Rangers   Archibald

Green Park
Ji Sung

ransfer Market

Kesington
(Olympiakos)

High Street
Kensingtony Mowbray

Micah Hyde Park Corner

Pico
Cercl

dstone Ground

Zat Knightsbridge

The Hammers

Dean
Court

Gloucester
City

St.James's
Park Ji Sung

Victoria Anichebe

ord Ravenscourt
e   Park Ji Sung

West
Kensingtony
Cottee

Earl
Barrett's
Court

South
Kensingtony
Gayle

Season-long
Loan Square

Taribo Wes

Re

West Brom

ns

hmond

Fulham 9

Pimlico Kranjcar

Nigel Pearsons Green

Watney Cup

Trevor Putney

eld Mill

Vauxhall
Conference

Wimbledon Park County

Wimbledon

Jamie Clanham No